MURDER AT YULETIDE

A 1920S COZY HISTORICAL MYSTERY

LEE STRAUSS

la plume
PRESS

Library and Archives Canada Cataloguing in Publication

Title: Murder at Yuletide / Lee Strauss.

Names: Strauss, Lee (Novelist), author.

Description: "A 1920s cozy historical mystery".

Identifiers: Canadiana (print) 2022044420X | Canadiana (ebook) 20220444218 | ISBN 9781774092392 (hardcover) | ISBN 9781774092422 (softcover) | ISBN 9781774092415 (IngramSpark softcover) | ISBN 9781774092385 (EPUB) | ISBN 9781774092408 (Kindle) Classification: LCC PS8637.T739 M87495 2023 | DDC C813/.6—dc23

*C*live Pippins held the note that had come for him in the morning post, his hand quivering. He had been in service since his sixteenth year —back in 1868—and until now, he'd never abandoned his post to run a personal errand.

Having grown up in a large family with a father who managed one of the farms belonging to a large estate, it was clear early on that the only way he could avoid the hard labour that came with farming or factory work was to find a position with a well-to-do family as a footman or bootboy. The estate steward noticed Pippins and took a liking to him as Clive Pippins had been born the amiable sort who liked to please. When a position became available at the house, the steward had recommended the eldest son of the Pippins family, and Clive had jumped at the chance.

Pippins stared at his hands, one of which still gripped the note. With their ropy blue veins, large knuckles, and loose, wrinkly skin, he didn't even recognise them. A look in the mirror was even more shocking. The old man who stared back had a shiny dome, blue eyes disappearing behind heavy hoods, and deep wrinkles with skin that seemed to fall loose from his face, mocking him. How had the years passed so quickly?

In those early days, Marchbold Manor was busy with many staff to serve the family upstairs. Besides the butler and housekeeper, there'd been a head cook, housemaids, and kitchen maids, along with footmen, and the earl's valet. A gardener and under-gardener managed the gardens whilst a groom and a coachman took care of the horses. The staff had worked together like a well-oiled machine and had become a family of sorts while they did it.

Eventually, Pippins had been promoted to underbutler. During those days, he'd fallen in love with the parlour maid, Susie, and she with him. They were happy for a brief time until the babe tried to come, and neither survived the effort. Those sad days were followed by Pippins' advancement in the ranks as he'd had nothing to aspire to apart from work, never wanting to subject his heart to that sort of ripping pain again.

Times changed, and big houses stopped employing as many servants as they used to. In fact, it was common for staff numbers to decrease even though one had to do the same work, if not more.

The earl had gently let Pippins know that he wouldn't be needed at the house anymore but that he knew of a man in the city looking for a butler, and would Pippins be willing to move to London?

It had been Pippins' fortieth year, 1892, and London sounded exciting and new. And most important, he'd be a butler for a prominent businessman and his wife, Mr. and Mrs. George Hartigan. It was a small house with a small staff, at least compared with what Pippins had known in the country, but it was sufficient.

Pippins sighed before stepping out from behind his desk in his small office. He'd ordered the wines and spirits that Mr. and Mrs. Reed had requested, ensuring plenty would be on hand for the Christmas season.

After conferring with Mrs. Beasley regarding lunch and dinner plans, Pippins would take care of menial tasks like polishing the silver, his ear attentive should the bell ring alerting him that Mr. or Mrs. Reed required his attention. Now at the end of 1927 his seventy-fifth year, he could still hear when a motorcar pulled up outside, or, if one preferred mysticism, he could feel the vibrations or the change in "energy".

The little dog was helpful, too. Mrs. Reed, the daughter of his first master, George Hartigan, liked to call the little canine Boss, but Pippins had difficulty voicing such a name to a family pet. He preferred the animal's full name of Boston, which he used now, the click-clacking of the Boston terrier's nails on the black-and-white tile announcing his approach.

"Boston," he said softly.

In former times, Pippins would've folded his tall body, bending deeply at the knees to lift the little dog into his arms and scratch him behind his pointy ears, but now he just nodded. The dog had done his part in announcing his mistress' arrival by letting out happy barks, and Pippins hurried to the entrance hall, smoothed out his suit and tails, and opened the door. Placing one arm behind his back, he reached out with the other—his gloves bleached a bright white—to take his mistress' coat and scarf.

"Thank you, Pips," Mrs. Reed said cheerily. She

looked radiant in a jade dress, her red hair perfectly coiffed and her green eyes bright with excitement. She brought a joy to the season that Pippins found contagious.

"You're welcome, madam." He bowed slightly.

Mrs. Reed was accompanied by her American friend Miss Haley Higgins, and Pippins offered to take her outerwear as well, though he was prepared for her refusal. Miss Higgins wasn't used to living with servants and often showed discomfort when others did what she was used to doing for herself.

This attitude was one of the many reasons service had changed, especially since the war. Modern times and modern thinking. These bright young things, as they were called, wanted to do things differently from their elders, but thankfully those of a higher class still liked to be waited on.

Miss Higgins took him up on his offer this time, and he moved away to hang the coats and scarves in the cloakroom. He glanced up at the enormous electric chandelier—the one bane of his existence. Hanging from the height of the upper floor, the fixture was challenging to dust. He had to arrange for Clement, who worked in the gardens and the stable, to bring in a large ladder for the maids to reach the fixture. The poor girls would complain bitterly about

5

hating heights. This apparent sleight of hand had to occur in the early mornings before the family members rose from their sleep.

"Pippins," Mrs. Reed said lightly. "Please arrange for tea and coffee in the sitting room. Thank you."

He waited for the ladies to disappear behind the tall French door, then immediately went to the kitchen to let Mrs. Beasley know about the request.

"I've just made fresh scones," the cook said. She was a funny-looking woman, nearly as wide as she was tall, but an expert at all things culinary. "I'll send Lizzie or Grace in with it; don't you worry."

"I need to step out for a short while," Pippins said.

Mrs. Beasley's eyes grew round. It was odd for Pippins to leave the house, at least while she was working, and if he did, he never made a point of saying so. Then she chuckled. "Oh, you're going to do a bit of Christmas shopping, eh? It's Christmas Eve tomorrow. Leaving it a bit tight, eh?"

Pippins hadn't been intending on shopping for gifts as he'd already bought chocolates for the women and cigars for the male staff. It would be impertinent to even think about buying for the family and their guest.

The folded note remained in his pocket, its writer beseeching him to meet him at Hatchards in the next hour. Should he find a book whilst there, perhaps he'd make a purchase so he didn't come back empty-handed. Mrs. Beasley had small eyes, but they worked like the dickens. If it weren't for the urgency implied, Pippins wouldn't even consider leaving.

"I shan't be long," he told the cook. "Lizzie can answer the door if necessary."

here was no time of year as loved by Ginger Reed—known by some as Lady Gold—as the Christmas season. It was close enough to Christmas that the pine aroma from the Christmas trees mingled with the scent of green boughs which decorated the staircase, cinnamon and spice from Mrs. Beasley's seasonal baking, and the smoky scent of the roaring fire in the stone fireplace in the sitting room where Ginger now found herself.

Though it was rainy and cold outside, inside, the atmosphere was cosy. There was the anticipation of gift giving and receiving and other lovely English traditions that Ginger was excited to share with Haley. Her American friend had recently arrived from Paris, where she'd been studying medicine.

Ginger's maid Lizzie brought a tray of coffee and tea, along with ginger nut biscuits, mince pies, and Scottish shortbread. Next to Haley sat Ginger's former sister-in-law, Felicia, Lady Davenport-Witt, and Felicia's grandmother, Ambrosia, the Dowager Lady Gold. Ginger delighted in the company.

"How long will you be staying, Miss Higgins?" Ambrosia's large bulbous eyes, encased in soft skin folds, narrowed. Unlike the "wild young girls of the age", she hadn't given up on the corset and sat upright with a stiff posture. Her grey hair was pulled back into a bun at her neck, a change from the previous decade when she'd still worn it piled high on her head, and her frock had found its way into the twentieth century with a looser waist and higher hemline that exposed narrow ankles. The long, crooked fingers of her right hand that gripped a silver-handled walking stick proudly displayed bejewelled rings. Ambrosia had never been a fan of "those who deny the throne", but Ginger was pleased to hear that the dowager's voice lacked the acerbic tone it often carried.

Haley wore a woollen suit with wide-leg trousers and a masculine-looking tie, her eyes flashing with intelligence and modern ideology. Ginger couldn't think of a person more diametrically opposite to

Ambrosia. Haley replied to the matriarch's question, "My studies continue in the new year, Lady Gold." Dark curls had escaped Haley's faux bob, and she pushed them off her face. "It's so kind of Ginger and your family to include me in your Christmas celebration this year."

"I can't believe we're almost in 1928," Felicia said after a sip of her tea. She shared Ginger's sense of style and general optimism. Her chestnut hair was styled in a voguish bob with shiny finger curls pinned off her face with sparkly hair clips. She wore an afternoon frock made of deep-purple velvet with a low velvet tie collar, a contrasting violet crêpe bodice and sleeve inlays, set off with a gold buckle at the hips. Felicia lifted her dainty chin, saying, "I can hardly wait to see what new excitement is in store for us all."

Ginger admired Felicia's effort to enter the joyous sentiments of the season. October had brought her and her husband Charles a terrible blow when Felicia miscarried her first pregnancy. At least on the outside, she seemed to have recovered, her chin high and her shoulders back. She'd confessed to Ginger she hadn't felt ready to take on the role of a mother and that perhaps Mother Nature knew best, but her bravado was diminished by the vulnerability in her eyes. Ginger knew how painful a loss like that was. In her first marriage, her miscarriage had happened so soon after she'd learned she was with child that it was as if it hadn't happened. A terrible dream she'd put behind her and rarely talked about.

"Charles and I are going to travel," Felicia continued. "It's something we talked about before we got married. We feel it's something we should do before our circumstances change again."

"That sounds exciting," Haley said as she cradled her coffee cup. "Where are you going to go?"

"South Africa, to start," Felicia said. "Steamships travel there and back to England regularly. I'd also like to go to India one day. I've heard it's very exotic."

"It sounds dangerous," Ambrosia said with a huff. "Surely, there must be enough to entertain you on British soil. Young people these days are never satisfied."

It was common for Felicia and her grandmother to misunderstand each other, which often turned into a battle of words accentuating the differences between their generations. But in this instance, Felicia offered rare insight into the source of Ambrosia's bitter tongue. "You needn't worry, Grandmama. Charles will protect me."

Ambrosia sniffed, then helped herself to a mince pie and nibbled.

"This is Rosa's first Christmas," Ginger said. "She senses that we're all excited about something, but the poor thing doesn't know what."

"When is your cousin joining us?" Felicia said. "You've hardly mentioned her."

"Florence is a third cousin of my father's." Ginger stared ahead blankly. "I've been amiss in not looking her up these last four years that I've been back in England. I'm quite ashamed of myself. She lives in Great Yarmouth, by the sea. It was Pippins who reminded me of her. I immediately invited her to come for Christmas if she had no other plans."

"What do we know of this Florence?" Ambrosia asked. "Does she have a surname?"

Ginger smiled. "Hartigan. Cousin Florence has never married."

"Since the war, that's been the plight of many ladies," Ambrosia said. "There aren't enough men to go around."

Ginger and Felicia shared a look. By God's grace, they were not counted amongst the many spinsters.

"She was already a spinster before the war," Ginger explained. "I believe she's in her fifth or sixth decade and quite comfortable with her status by now."

"What is her connection with Pippins?" Haley asked.

"Papa loaned Pippins to Cousin Enid during the war years when Hartigan House was closed down. A good decade. Poor Enid passed away before he got there, and her sister Florence became mistress of the house." Ginger worked her lips as she mused. "I imagine it was hard for Cousin Florence to give him up after so much time. I never gave it much thought when he returned to Hartigan House."

"I imagine she found another butler who worked as well," Ambrosia said.

Ginger wondered if the dowager had ever grown close to any of her staff. She certainly counted on Langley, but Ginger had never seen Ambrosia exhibit any sign of affection towards her lady's maid.

"What does she do up in Great Yarmouth?" Felicia asked. "It must be so dull."

"Some people like the quiet of a smaller town," Ginger said. "And the solace of the seaside."

Haley rose to stoke the fire, and Ambrosia shot Ginger a questioning look as if to say, *Why does your American friend insist on doing the maid's work?*

Oblivious to the exchange, Haley said, "I look

forward to meeting her. One single lady to another. I'm sure we'll have a lot to commiserate over."

Ambrosia turned a flummoxed look away from Haley. "When is she arriving?" Ambrosia asked Ginger.

"She's already in London," Ginger replied. "She said she preferred to take a hotel room. I suspect our numbers are too great and that a spinster used to being alone more than not would find it intimidating. She'll join us tomorrow for Christmas Eve and again on Christmas morning. I must check with Pippins regarding the exact time."

Once the tea and coffee had been consumed, Ambrosia excused herself, ringing Langley to help her upstairs to her room. Felicia also said her good-byes and headed across Mallowan Court to her house. Before her wedding, Felicia had lived at Hartigan House, and Ginger had missed her when she left. She considered it a blessing when the Davenport-Witts had taken another house on the court.

"I think I'll take a bit of time to withdraw to my room," Haley said. "Even though I'm on holidays, I still have reading to do."

"Of course," Ginger said. "I'll see you at dinner."

Ginger headed up the staircase to check up on

Rosa in the nursery and to look for Scout. Rosa reached out her chubby arms when she spotted Ginger, and Ginger swooped her up.

"Poor thing's cheeks are so red," she said before kissing them.

"There's another tooth coming in, madam," Nanny Green said. "I've got a bit of ice in a cloth for her to suck on. It seems to help."

Ginger rocked Rosa in her arms, stroking the child's dark hair until she fell asleep, then handed her back to the nanny. She returned downstairs through the vast entryway, her heels tapping on the tile. She searched for her son Scout to ensure the lad was staying out of trouble, or at least out of the kitchen and Mrs. Beasley's way, and also for Pippins, to ask him about Florence Hartigan.

The kitchen was filled with the aroma of Mrs. Beasley's baking. Scout was there eating ginger biscuits and drinking a glass of milk. Boss sat on his haunches at Scout's feet, waiting for sweet crumbs to come his way.

Mrs. Beasley and Grace, the kitchen maid, were bustling about. Hartigan House boasted a large and modern kitchen. A long rectangular worktable with shelves beneath and an army of pots and pans hanging from the ceiling above were in the middle of the room, and Lizzie as well as Grace was helping Mrs. Beasley by chopping winter vegetables. A deep porcelain sink sat under the garden window where Mrs. Beasley grew herbs year-round. There was an oversized cast-iron coal-burning stove, but Ginger's pride—and Mrs. Beasley's delight—was the new monitor-top refrigerator. A stainless-steel four-legged cabinet was the size of a large safe. Painted shiny white, it had a compressor on the top that resembled a gun turret. After its arrival, Mrs. Beasley's round face had been stamped with a huge smile for weeks.

When Scout had first come to Hartigan House, it was to help Mrs. Beasley. After Ginger and Basil had adopted him, the lad was put into a position of superiority. It had taken some time for everyone in the house to adjust. Still, Ginger was thankful that the rough period between the cook and her son seemed to have ended.

"Have you seen Pippins?" Ginger asked. From Ginger's perspective, Pips had a magical quality of always appearing when she required him, as if he had a sixth sense when it came to her needs. It was unusual for her to have to seek him out.

Mrs. Beasley scratched her nose, leaving a patch of flour behind. "He's gone out, madam." She winked. "I think he's behind with his Christmas shopping."

"Oh, I see," Ginger said, though she didn't. It was unlike Pippins to leave the house during working hours. "Please ask him to find me when he returns."

"Yes, madam," Mrs. Beasley said with an awkward shallow curtsy.

"Don't eat too many," Ginger said to Scout. "You'll make yourself ill."

Scout's lips turned up into a sheepish grin. "Yes, Mummy."

3

*D*espite wearing long woollen long johns, trousers, and a woollen vest under an even thicker wool coat, Pippins found he could never save his warmth in the damp and cold British winters. With the thick muffler Mrs. Beasley had knitted him as a gift the previous Christmas wrapped around his swooping neck and a bowler hat pressed down on his bald head, he leaned towards the taxicab driver, wishing the man could get his machine to move along a little more quickly.

"There's a bit of traffic today, eh?"

"It's nearly Christmas," the driver said. "So many motorcars are on the streets. And with this blasted rain . . ." He swerved sharply to miss a new pothole, throwing Pippins off balance in the back.

A feeling of invincibility seemed to come over drivers, and Pippins felt that one nearly took one's life in one's hands when agreeing to be a passenger. Pippins didn't like to be uncharitable, but Mrs. Reed's lovely face came to mind.

They turned on to Piccadilly, rumbling down the street with the tired winter-brown lawns of Green Park to the right and a view of Buckingham Palace peeking through leafless trees in the distance, a blurry rendition viewed through the rivulets of rain running down the window.

When the taxicab finally came to a stop at number 187, Pippins dropped coins into the driver's outreached hand. Hatchards bookshop was the place to go in London for any book, magazine, or paper product. Hatchards had been a name in publishing and in the city of London for over a hundred years.

The facade was made of darkly stained wood which framed two large windows displaying the latest releases. A wooden sign stretched along the width of the shop overhead with the words, "HATCHARDS: Booksellers to the King." Another sign read, "Established 1797." Older than he was, Pippins mused, by fifty-five years.

Inside, a shopper would be met with the comforting smell of newly printed ink on paper, the musky smell of wood oil, and despite the char-woman's best efforts, dust. Pippins was pleased a fire burned brightly in the fireplace—the warmth both inviting and charming.

"Welcome to Hatchards."

As he removed it, Pippins tipped his hat at the woman who stood behind the counter, her job to greet customers as they entered and to take the money from them for their purchases when they left.

Rows of shelves filled more than one floor, and with hundreds of books, one could lose hours perusing the titles, reading dust covers and first chapters, and deliberating about what to purchase. Christmas shoppers huddled around the shelves lined with fiction titles, with a few mothers choosing books that aided children in learning.

Few people were in the travel section, and only one was to be found in the back with the world atlases, a lady in a navy-blue embroidered coat with a dark fur collar and white gloves, looking more nervous than was natural for a person in search of a book.

"Good afternoon, Pippins," she said as he approached. Florence Hartigan had never been a beautiful woman, but she had fine-enough features. Her hair was nearly grey, and even though Pippins had seen her only a few months before, he still thought of her as a brunette, the way she was when they had first met.

Pippins, his hat in hand, gave a slight bow. "Miss Hartigan. It's a pleasure to see you again."

"Yes, thank you for coming, Pippins. I know my summons was rather unorthodox."

"Can I assume you've had another, er . . ." Pippins glanced about the shop to ensure no one was near enough to hear him. A shop worker, dressed in a single-breasted, grey pin-striped suit, stood with his hands behind his back, scanning the shop, perhaps to prevent the success of possible shoplifters or to assist a customer with a question. His eyes caught Pippins', and Pippins looked away. "You've had another missive?"

"Indeed. That's why I'm here at this shop. My tormentor wants to continue with the game. I'm to search for a particular book to find further instructions." Miss Hartigan let out a heavy sign. "I'm sorry, Pippins. I shouldn't involve you in my difficulties. It's not as if I can't find the book on my own."

"You've been put in a distressing position, madam," Pippins said. "I'm happy to offer my support in any way."

Miss Hartigan wrung her hands together. "It

really is a nuisance! It's so tiresome to be looking over one's shoulder, dreading the daily post. I just want to return to normal living, with no ghosts or surprises."

Pippins also wished that for his former employer but was at a loss as to how to bring that to pass. His suggestion to tell Mr. and Mrs. Reed about her problem had been quickly and severely shut down. He hoped that once Miss Hartigan had got to know her relatives over Christmas, she'd see that she could trust them and would seek their help.

Pippins nodded to Miss Hartigan's handbag. "What does this one say?"

Miss Hartigan opened her handbag and withdrew a paper folded in thirds. She flattened it out and handed it to Pippins. "You can read it for yourself."

Pippins frowned as he read, then folded the paper and handed it back to Miss Hartigan. "I concur that you are in the right section. I gather we're looking for an older atlas. Shall I ask for assistance?"

"No." Miss Hartigan returned the letter to her handbag. "I can't risk that someone else might see something they shouldn't."

"Very well," Pippins said. "Let us look."

The current atlases were red-bound books

called *The New World Atlas and Gazetteer;* Pippins and Miss Hartigan flipped pages, only to find nothing.

"'*At Times, vast foreign countries, where no one abides,*'" Miss Hartigan said reciting from the riddle. "The word *Times* was oddly capitalised. Perhaps it's in the title."

"Indeed," Pippins said. "There's an atlas in the Hartigan House library from the first decade of the century published by *The Times.* Perhaps there is a copy here." The older atlas proved elusive indeed, and if it hadn't been for Pippins' height—though he was no longer as tall as he'd been in his prime—they might've missed seeing it.

"It's here," Pippins said, but when he went to remove the book, Miss Hartigan commanded that he stop.

"Let me," she said. "I should do it." She pushed the wooden ladder that ran along a railing attached to the top of the bookshelf until it reached the spot where Pippins stood.

He stepped to the side, letting the lady retrieve the book, even though he could've easily reached it for her. She wanted to be the first to see whatever message she feared might be hidden in the book.

Miss Hartigan pushed her handbag so it hung

over her shoulder, gripped the ladder, and despite wearing a frock, stepped up three rungs.

Pippins stood closely behind her so he could assist should she misstep. "Do be careful, madam."

Releasing one side of the ladder, Miss Hartigan reached above her head, gripped the book by its spine, and slid it from its spot on the shelf. A couple of adjacent books came out with it and clattered to the floor.

"Dear me," she said, her face etched with dismay.

"Don't worry, madam," Pippins said. He tugged on his trousers and carefully lowered himself to reach for the first book.

Pippins hadn't even got his fingers on it when a loud explosion blasted his ears, and he was thrown to the floor in darkness.

hief Inspector Basil Reed worked for the love of the job. Raised in privilege, he could've chosen the life of a gentleman of leisure, and he might have, had it not been for the outbreak of the war. The Great War had been a stark revelation. When one's country was under attack, all men became equals. For the first time in his life, he had felt like he had a purpose, that his life had a deeper meaning than how he wanted his eggs for breakfast and if he should go shooting or play a round of golf.

His time at the front had been short-lived, as he had taken a bullet in his first skirmish. He lost his spleen and his dignity, being sent back to London to wait out the war with the women and children.

It was how he had ended up at the Metropolitan Police. Though crime was low during the war, the streets still needed watching, and putting his time in with the police was his way of doing his bit.

And not only was he good at it, but he also liked it. Policing and detecting gave him a reason to get up in the morning, especially when his first marriage broke down. The job had given him a place to go and something to occupy his mind. He'd been doing the job for over ten years with no plans to stop. The only irritation was having an oaf like Morris as his boss. The man saw himself as the engine of the train when, in fact, he was the brake van at the end. Everyone could see that, except the superintendent himself, who'd been gifted the job because of his relationship with the Lord Mayor and had few skills to carry out his responsibilities.

"Reed!" Morris' voice was like a megaphone, and Basil couldn't pretend not to have heard it. With a sigh, he lifted himself from his desk, abandoned his paperwork, and walked to Morris' office.

"Sir," he said as he stepped inside.

"Have you arranged for someone to play Father Christmas at the Marchioness of Greenbrough's children's party tonight? In fact, you best take the role yourself. And take some extra men along; they can be Father Christmas' helpers."

"Sir?" Basil responded with a note of incredulousness. "Do you really think this is the best use of the force's time and resources?"

"The Marchioness of Greenbrough is an important patroness of the Yard. She sent an excellent bottle of Napoleon brandy as a token of her appreciation. It would never do to offend her."

Basil bit his tongue. There was no way on God's green earth he would agree to such a charade, and he'd even pretend to be ill or claim a family emergency to avoid it. Thankfully, Braxton's voice, calling for him, saved him from saying something he might regret.

"Sir," Braxton said.

The constable wore a standard dark blue police uniform with a row of brass buttons. "We've got word of an explosion in Piccadilly. At the bookshop."

Basil shot Morris a look. The man seemed put out by this sudden inconvenience but waved him off. "Go on, then."

The constable jogged towards Basil's office. "I'll get your hat and coat, sir."

Before long, Basil and Braxton were headed out

in a police motorcar with Braxton at the wheel through the steady downpour.

"An explosion at Hatchards?" Basil asked. "Is there a fire?"

"The copper in the area said smoke only. And injuries. Possibly a death. An ambulance is on the way."

Basil's mind searched for all the possible causes of an explosion to happen at a bookshop. The Bolsheviks had been a recent source of trouble, and Basil wondered if it might be another form of terror from them, though a bookshop attack would be curious.

Braxton pulled the motorcar to a stop at the kerb in front of the shop. From the street, nothing looked out of the ordinary except for the crowd of people loitering outside despite the rain and cold. The ambulance was there already.

Placing his trilby firmly on his head, Basil stepped out of the motorcar. "Make way," he said. "Police."

Inside, he was greeted by a man who wrung his hands, frowning at his surroundings as he tutted his disbelief. Dust from the explosion had filtered to the front of the store, and books lay on the wooden floor. A woman behind the counter softly sobbed as she huddled in a chair.

"I'm Douglas Jennings," the man said. "I'm the shop manager."

"Please take me to the scene, Mr. Jennings."

"Yes, sir." The man led them to the opening of what had once been an aisle between bookshelves, with an apparent dead end. Damaged and destroyed books were scattered everywhere, wooden shelves were broken and splintered, and two bodies on the floor, a male and a female, had been dug out from under the debris.

"What section was this?" Basil asked.

"Er, one side of the row is the history section. The shelves on the back wall housed travel books and atlases. It's not exactly the most popular section when it comes to Christmas shopping. I try to keep an eye on all the areas but was paying more attention to the folks in the front—Shakespeare and Sherlock Holmes are favourite choices—when suddenly there was a boom. Sounded like a bomb going off." He glanced sideways with a sheepish look. "I wasn't the only soldier to drop to the ground, sir. Brought back memories of the war, it did."

"Thank you, Mr. Jennings," Basil said. "That will be all for now. Please remain in the shop should I have further questions."

The manager's expression darkened at the request, but he did as he was bid.

Basil turned his attention to the doctor at the scene, a man Basil hadn't met before. London was home to several hospitals and countless doctors, and Basil didn't expect to know everyone. The doctor seemed to be in his thirties with a sharp side parting combed and oiled with precision. He squatted by the injured man on the floor and glanced up at Basil with serious eyes before returning to his task.

"I'm Chief Inspector Reed," Basil said.

The doctor stood and reached out to shake Basil's hand. "Dr. Palmer." He waved to the body on the floor. "We have a fatality and a severe injury. The woman was dead when I got here. From the burns on her face, I'm presuming she took the brunt of the blast. This elderly gentleman, by some miracle, still has a pulse, but he needs hospital care immediately."

The commotion behind Basil and Braxton proved to be two ambulance attendants coming in with a stretcher. Basil got a good look at his face when they lifted the injured man off the ground. "Good Lord. That's Pippins."

"You know him, sir?" Braxton asked.

"That's our butler." Basil's eyes darted to the

deceased on the floor, his heart dropping. Scanning the debris, he spotted what looked like a lady's handbag, blackened with smoke. Opening it, he found the identification he was looking for. "It's Mrs. Reed's cousin, Miss Hartigan."

"Sir?" Braxton said, his face flashing with uncertainty. "Would you like me to contact Mrs. Reed?"

"Yes. Go to the house and bring her here."

The constable had worked on enough cases with Basil to know that Ginger would insist on coming anyway and left without further question.

Dr. Palmer lifted a clean-shaven chin. "I'm assuming you'd like the body to remain whilst you do your preliminary investigation. I'll send the ambulance back to retrieve it in an hour."

"Very good," Basil said. Removing his overcoat, he carefully laid it over the body out of respect. Then he turned his attention back to the scene, staring quizzically at the indentation in the exterior wall. A cold, wet wind blew inside through an inset in the brickwork. On closer inspection, the top edges of several insets peeked out from the pieces of the shelving still attached to the brick wall.

Basil called out to one of the officers standing by. "Constable Cole!"

"Yes, sir?" Cole said.

"Contact the Yard and request a bomb expert."

The constable responded with enthusiasm. "Yes, sir!"

Basil knew it was a long shot for the Yard to track down a bomb expert at short notice and before Christmas, but with the war in the not-too-distant past, there were undoubtedly enough men who'd qualify as experts in London. Perhaps he'd be lucky.

Even with his lack of qualification, Basil could tell that the circumference of the blast was twelve to fifteen feet, and it had had a force that was strong enough to knock over the heavy shelves opposite the wall, scatter books about, and tear pages, ripping them from the binding.

Miss Hartigan's body had also been thrown. Pippins had fallen closer to the wall. A metal fragment caught Basil's eye, and he reached for it with his gloved hand. A piece of the explosive device? He dropped it into the paper evidence bag he'd brought. Sifting through the debris on the floor, he came across other pieces of shrapnel, mostly metal but also a splinter of wood about a foot long and a section of torched cording.

Basil grunted as he stood, stretching out the kink in his back. His guess was a hand bomb, triggered by the tugging of the cord, perhaps as the book was removed from the shelf.

The question here was less of how, but why? Were Pippins and Miss Hartigan just unlucky victims of terror? Or had they been specifically targeted?

5

*W*hen Constable Braxton arrived at Hartigan House to deliver his message about an explosion at Hatchards and that Basil had asked for her assistance, Ginger wasted no time responding. "Was anyone hurt?"

"Yes, madam. One injury and one fatality."

Haley wasn't about to be left behind. She grabbed her doctor's bag and an umbrella before rushing out the back entrance to the garden. She helped Ginger open the garage doors, the gardener, Clement, hurrying to help when he saw them.

"I don't know why we didn't go with the constable in the police motorcar," Haley said.

"I like to have my own transportation," Ginger replied as she slid into the leathered-leather seat on the driver's side of her pearly-white 1924 Crossley Sports Tourer. "One never knows what one might need to do next."

Ginger didn't understand why Haley was such a nervous passenger but wrote it off as not being used to the traffic operating on the left side instead of the right as they splashed through the heavy rain.

Piccadilly wasn't so far from South Kensington, and with some creative driving, which had elicited a few shocking swear words from Haley, Ginger brought her Crossley to a stop near the bookshop. An officer stood guard at the door, periodically stomping his feet to ward off the cold and shooing away potential shoppers or nosy parkers. He raised a head to warn them away, but his expression softened when he recognised Ginger.

"Mrs. Reed. The chief inspector is expecting you." He cast a wary glance at Haley.

"This is Nurse Higgins," Ginger said. "She's with me."

The constable opened the door and let them inside. Another uniformed officer stood guard at the front of the shop, waiting with two people Ginger guessed might be witnesses.

"He's in the back area, madam," the officer said, walking ahead to lead them.

Ginger was stunned by the damage. "Basil?"

"Ginger," Basil said as he approached. "Haley. I'm glad you came along."

"Of course," Haley said.

Ginger followed her friend's gaze to the body lying on the floor.

"Shall I?" Haley said.

"Please do." Staring at Ginger with hazel eyes soft with compassion, Basil took Ginger's hand. "I'm afraid it's Florence Hartigan."

Ginger blinked hard as she processed the news, her feet moving around Basil to Haley's side, seeing the truth of Basil's words as Haley lifted the overcoat off the body, which was clearly female, the embroidered coat, charred and tattered. The lady had lost her hat, and her short hair stood out like it had been caught in a surge of electricity. The skin on her face was bruised and burned, but not so much that Ginger didn't notice the familial resemblance.

Ginger's gloved hand went to her throat. "Oh mercy."

"I'm very sorry, love," Basil said kindly.

"Poor dear," Ginger said. "And we didn't even get a chance to get to know one another."

"She has burns on her face," Haley said, "several contusions evident through the tears in her clothing.

There are more contusions on her back, which are likely a result of a fall to the floor."

Ginger slumped. "I do hope she died quickly."

Haley cast a sympathetic smile. "She wouldn't have known what hit her."

Basil pointed to a charred and broken ladder. "I believe she was on this contraption, reaching for a book on a higher shelf. You can see the source of the explosion came from that blackened hole."

Ginger's mind raced for a possible cause of such an event. She narrowed her eyes at Basil. "A hand bomb?"

Basil nodded. "I believe so. I've gathered what I believe is bomb debris, and the rest I'll have properly gathered and taken into evidence. Hopefully, we can piece together the make and possibly even the source."

"Someone went to the trouble to booby-trap a particular book?" Ginger said incredulously. "And Cousin Florence just happened to select it today?"

Haley stood, brushing off her tweed skirt as she did. "That seems a bit too coincidental to me."

"Sir?"

Ginger turned with Basil at the sound of the constable's voice. "Your bomb expert is here."

"Splendid!" Basil grinned crookedly at Ginger. "A Christmas miracle."

A short, rotund man with ruddy cheeks and a perky white moustache stood at the scene's periphery and whistled. "Someone's not 'avin' a 'appy Christmas."

"No indeed," Basil said. "I'm Chief Inspector Reed; this is my wife, Mrs. Reed, and her friend Miss Higgins."

The bomb expert lifted a shoulder, thick under his heavy trench coat, as if he wondered what the two ladies were doing in such a setting, but to his credit, he made no remark. He removed his hat and said, "A pleasure. Walter Latham at your service."

"Mr. Latham," Basil started. "Thank you for coming at short notice and so close to Christmas."

"No problem at all," he said with a chuckle. "I was 'appy for an excuse to get out the 'ouse. I've got a nosy ma and too many screamin' grandkids at 'ome."

Ginger shared an amused look with Basil before asking, "I assume your expertise comes from your service during the war?"

"It does indeed, madam. And from the looks of things, I can tell yer straight away that yer dealin' with a 'and bomb. Short blast circumference. I won't trample your scene, but I think I can see from 'ere where the bomb was planted." He pointed to the damaged inset in the brickwork. "Right up there."

"I believe you're right," Basil said.

From the scorching around the heavily damaged bricks, Ginger had to agree.

"What did yer find for debris?" Mr. Latham asked.

Basil held out a bag. "I've collected everything I could find, at least at first glance. I'll have the lads do a finer search. You'll be able to review this in the evidence room at the Yard."

"Very good, sir," Mr. Latham said. He raised a busy brow. "Perhaps I'll call the day after Boxin' Day? I'd rather not upset the missus if I can 'elp it."

Ginger could tell by the twitch in Basil's jaw that he'd be happy to deliver both the evidence and Mr. Latham to Scotland Yard that very day, but he lifted his chin and said, "I'm sure that would be fine."

Mr. Latham nodded as he extended wishes for a happy Christmas and went on his way. The ambulance attendants must've crossed him in the shop as they arrived just seconds after Mr. Latham left.

Haley took charge of that situation, using her body to shield the view of poor Florence from Ginger's line of sight. Once the body was on the stretcher and properly covered with a sheet, Haley said, "I'll accompany the body to the hospital. Maybe I can be of assistance."

Basil lifted a handbag from the ground and offered it to Ginger. "It's Miss Hartigan's. I don't enjoy going through a lady's handbag, but it was necessary. There's a letter inside."

Ginger took the handbag and fished out the letter.

> My spine is stiff, my poetry stale
> I'm as old as these streets
> I tell many a tale
> There's one about oceans with
>   no tide
> Vast foreign countries, where no one
>   abides.

"A riddle?" Ginger loved a good riddle. "*My spine is stiff, my poetry stale,* could refer to an out-of-date book. *I'm as old as these streets* . . . well, Hatchards was the oldest bookstore in London, and the reference to oceans and countries would bring her to the travel section."

Ginger glanced at the stretcher carrying her cousin's body out of the room. "Dear Cousin Florence. What did you get yourself mixed up in?"

"Her and Pippins," Basil said.

Ginger spun and locked eyes with her husband. "What does Pippins have to do with it?"

"Didn't Braxton tell you?"

"Tell me what, Basil?"

"Pippins was here with Florence Hartigan."

"*He*'s the injured person?" Ginger sprinted away with Basil after her. "I'm going to the hospital," she yelled back. "You can find me there."

6

*G*inger's mind was foggier than the low-lying pea-soup fog that London was famous for. Poor Pips! Her stomach churned as she imagined the injury he must've incurred, especially seeing how the explosion had damaged Cousin Florence. Ginger viewed Clive Pippins as a sturdy man whose skills had improved with age. When, on occasion, she'd acknowledged his age—nearing eighty, poor thing—her heart clutched with premature grief. Pippins had been a fixture of her childhood when his head had hair, and he called her "Little Miss". Around the staff, he was unflappable, standing tall and speaking with authority, but with her, he softened like a jolly grandfather.

When her father had taken her to America as a

child, she had shed heartfelt tears over losing Pippins more than for her stiff governess, who'd simply seen her as the subject of her employment. After a solemn goodbye, Ginger had never heard from the governess nor given her another thought. But she'd never lost fondness for Pippins. Their reunion in '23, after the Great War, was the first happy thing that had happened to her after her return to London.

Vaguely aware that her journey, slowed by the inability of her windscreen wipers to deal with the heavy rain, had been accentuated with a melody of honking horns and random shouts, she'd finally arrived at St Bartholomew's Hospital.

Slightly out of breath, she stopped in front of the reception desk nurse, asked for Pip's room number, and then hurried there as fast as her T-strapped shoes would take her. Ginger paused at the open door of Pippins' room and gasped. Her butler's bald head was nearly concealed by the mound of bandages. His eyes were closed, and dark circles beneath them were a bruised nightshade-purple. His breath was raspy through dry, parted lips. The nurse had told her that the ulna in his left arm had been fractured. It was in a splint, waiting on the doctors to create a cast.

The nurses had propped him up on two pillows

to assist his alarmingly shallow breathing. Ginger stepped up to the bed and cupped his cool, frail hand in hers. "Pippins. I'm here." To her delight, his eyelids fluttered at the sound of her voice, staying open long enough to glance at her briefly before falling shut again.

"Miss," he said.

Ginger blinked. He'd called her Miss. As in Little Miss, perhaps? The poor man had banged his head. It would be natural if he couldn't think clearly.

"You're going to be all right," Ginger said. "Don't you worry about a thing."

Pippins' lips pulled up in a soft smile, the lines around his eyes deepening as if he recalled a humorous image. "A man broke into Buckingham Palace."

Ginger raised a brow. Poor Pippins was incoherent. The fact that he wanted to speak had to be a good sign. She patted his hand. "Why would he do that?"

"He wanted to talk to King George. He scaled the iron fence, sneaked past the palace guard, and entered through a basement window. Imagine that!"

Ginger recalled the event. It had been reported in *The New York Times*, and Ginger had recited the story to her father over tea in June 1914. Henry Pike, a motor engineer with a grievance, had slipped over the palace fence and past the guards before entering through a palace window. He'd found a cupboard containing staff uniforms and had changed into one, then stolen a silver cigarette case and a walking stick. The situation's absurdity and the apparent lack of palace security had been the headline for days.

Pippins continued in his laboured and raspy voice. "Liverpool Street station was so lively and crowded, and it took me some doing to find platform nine."

"Platform nine?" Ginger said. A German bomb had hit that platform in '17.

"The Great Eastern Railway Line," Pippins said. "It links to Norwich and then on to Great Yarmouth."

Florence Hartigan had lived in Great Yarmouth, where Pippins had worked from 1914 until 1923. He left his employ there to return to his duties at Hartigan House when Ginger had returned to London. Ginger studied her butler's face. Why was he telling her this?

"The Willows is smaller than Hartigan House, but my duties are similar, overseeing the main floor, the wine cellar, and ensuring that the pantry is properly stocked."

Ginger noted that Pippins had changed to the present tense. Her chest tightened. Had his head injury caused a form of amnesia?

"It's so different from city life, isn't it, miss? Quiet except for the crashing shore and those blasted birds crowing unceasingly. It's what one would call quaint, isn't it? It has stuccoed brick walls, a hipped tile roof, and a gabled porch. And those two Doric pilasters flanking the front entrance."

"It sounds charming," Ginger replied. She regretted that she hadn't had the opportunity to visit.

"I still dream of those days," Pippins said. Weakly, he squeezed Ginger's hand. "And of meeting you."

Ginger frowned at Pippins' apparent confusion. "Which days, Pippins?"

"Perhaps . . ." Pippins' voice broke off into a dry cough. A glass of water sat on the bedside table, and Ginger reached for it, lifting it to his lips as she helped to prop up his head.

"Have a sip," she said.

The water seemed to do its job of calming the man. He needed his rest, but since he'd been rather talkative, she thought she'd take a chance and asked, "Pippins, what happened at the bookshop?"

Pippins' eyes fluttered as his chest rose and fell, and the soft snoring from light sleep emanated.

She stayed with him as he slept, holding his hand, determined to stay until the doctor came to check on him. That he was still alive was enough for her, for now. She feared what the doctor might say and was in no hurry to hear it.

Pippins jerked and talked in his sleep. "We could've done things differently, eh?" he said. "But what, Miss Hartigan? What?"

"What, Pippins?" Ginger prompted. "What could you have done differently?"

Pippins' eyes twitched under his thin eyelids, apparently falling deeper into his dream, leaving Ginger's questions unanswered.

7

*I*f Basil hadn't repeatedly reassured her that the hospital would ring the moment Pippins was in need, Ginger would've skipped the family breakfast to be at her butler's side.

"It's Christmas Eve," Basil said. "Pippins is in good hands and sleeping. I've already rung myself. Enjoy breakfast, then go if you must."

Ginger sighed as she relented. "Of course. It's going to be so odd not having Pippins to watch over us."

Shedding her feather-trimmed nightclothes, Ginger dressed in a long blue-and-grey blouse with a geometrical motif over a grey pleated skirt. A narrow black belt lay low on the hips. She could've called on Lizzie to help, but that would be awkward with Basil in the room. Besides, he didn't mind giving her a hand when she needed it. He demonstrated a keen intuition when it came to her, standing at the ready to fasten the button at the back of her neck and to fuss with the clasp of her silver necklace.

"Thank you, love," she said.

Basil turned her around to face him, his hazel eyes glistening with fondness. "Happy Christmas, darling," he said before kissing her gently.

Walking together in the corridor, hand in hand like young lovers, they called in at the nursery to see Rosa, taking turns kissing the toddler's round red cheeks and running fingers through her silky dark curls.

"I've got her ready for the day," Nanny Green said. "I will stay the night, as I usually do, but I'm taking the underground in the morning. My family is expecting me for Christmas dinner."

Ginger smiled at Basil. "We can manage one small child for an evening, can't we?"

Basil smirked. "I presume so."

After both took time to hold and play with their infant daughter, they knocked on Scout's bedroom door. "Breakfast, Scout," Ginger called.

The door immediately opened. Scout, a lean, diminutive fifteen-year-old boy with straw-coloured hair and a maturing complexion, stepped into the corridor. Having experienced hunger as a child, Scout never dallied when it came to mealtimes. Now, as a youth, he exercised a carefree attitude, stuffing his fists into his pockets as he languidly followed his parents downstairs.

Usually, breakfast was served in the morning room, but for this special Christmas Eve, the meal had been set up in the dining room. In one of the last rooms Ginger redecorated after moving from Boston, she had kept the intricately carved, long wooden table and chairs but added an electric chandelier to hang overhead. The dark colours on the wall had been replaced with brighter lemon wallpaper printed with geometrical shapes.

Ambrosia and Haley were already there, and by the look of relief on Haley's face, she was happy for others to contribute to whatever conversation had been taking place. Ginger was itching with curiosity. After dishing up their plates from the array on the sideboard—kidneys, kippers, bacon, and eggs—they returned to the table.

"What have we missed?" Ginger said.

Basil pulled out a chair for her, then took the one nearest to her at the head of the table.

"Miss Higgins admits to going to the bookshop

with you," Ambrosia said, "but refuses to answer my questions. Don't I have a right to know what is going on?"

"I did answer your questions, Lady Gold," Haley said, rolling her eyes towards Ginger. "The ones I know the answers to."

Ambrosia caught Ginger's eye. "She says your Cousin Florence died in an explosion? What on earth could explode at a bookshop?"

Ginger and Haley both understood that the police withheld information from the public if they thought doing so might aid in the investigation. The explosion was publicly known, but only Basil, Ginger, and Haley, along with a select few at Scotland Yard, knew about the hand bomb and the enigmatic letter found in Florence's handbag.

"The investigation is ongoing," Basil said. "It's most definitely foul play; however, we can't really say more than that."

Ambrosia snorted her derision. "Such insufferable hubris. Who's to say I wouldn't be of help? She was to be a guest at this table."

Ginger made a point of looking at Scout, hoping to suggest that the lad was the reason they had to watch what they said. Ambrosia was to accept it and allow them to change the subject. It was rather unfair to Scout, who caught the look and frowned. Ambrosia followed the exchange and harrumphed. She'd never warmed to Scout rising from the ranks of street waif to kitchen help to Ginger's adopted son. She turned with a finger raised and scowled. "Where is Pippins?"

"Oh, Grandmother," Ginger said. "Pippins was at the bookshop when the explosion went off. He's convalescing in hospital."

Ambrosia dropped her fork. "See? *This* is what I mean. Why was I not informed? I do despise being treated like a useless old lady."

"The oversight was unintentional," Basil replied.

Felicia and Charles arrived, and Ginger said, "Finally," as she rose to her feet. She embraced Felicia first, then Charles. "Lovely to see you."

Felicia returned the sentiment, though her usual cheer hadn't entered her eyes. Losing a child was difficult but especially hard on the heart at Christmas. "We had to face a monsoon crossing the street," Felicia said.

Ginger stared out the window and saw the rain coming down in sheets. "Is it still as cold as it was yesterday?"

Felicia shivered. "Yes. It's frightfully cold!'"

After greeting everyone else, the Davenport-

Witts served themselves from the sideboard and took a seat. Ginger rang the bell for a fresh pot of tea.

Ambrosia homed in on her granddaughter. "Did you know about Pippins, Felicia?"

Felicia flicked a napkin and laid it on her lap. "Know what?" She glanced about the room, searching for him. "Where is he? Is he all right? I wondered why Lizzie dealt with our dripping wet coats and umbrellas."

Ambrosia relaxed in her chair, apparently appeased that she wasn't the only one not to know.

"He was injured in that blast at the bookshop," Ginger said. "And sadly, Cousin Florence was killed."

Felicia's mouth dropped open. "What? Your cousin who was to come for Christmas?"

"I'm afraid so," Ginger said.

"Oh," Charles said. "It was she who perished? I read about it in the morning paper."

"How peculiar," Felicia said. "Imagine coming to London to visit family for Christmas and dying in such a random way?"

Ginger shared a look with Haley and Basil, but none of them mentioned that they feared it wasn't all that random.

Felicia reached for Ginger's hand. "Are you all right? This must be such a shock."

"The greater shock is that Pippins was hurt," Ginger said. "I never knew Cousin Florence. Pippins is more like family to me than she was."

"He's not terribly hurt," Felicia said. "Is he?"

Ginger nibbled her lip. "I hope not," she finally said. "I was with him at the hospital yesterday. He was rather incoherent. I think he thought I was Cousin Florence."

Haley held Ginger's gaze. "Confusion and delirium aren't uncommon with a head injury."

"He hit his head?" Charles asked, tapping his finger on a chair.

"The explosion threw him to the floor," Basil said. "The doctors think he suffered a concussion."

"But he'll recover from that, won't he?" Felicia said. Her concern would have been endearing if it weren't laced with panic. Ginger looked at Haley before squeezing Felicia's arm. "Pippins is elderly but strong. We can hope and pray for the best, dear."

"Are we going to get a new butler?"

Scout had been so quiet, and everyone so focused on Felicia and her fragile state, that he'd been momentarily forgotten.

"We don't need to think about that now," Ginger said.

"Why on earth not?" Ambrosia countered. "A house like this needs a reliable butler."

"And what do you suggest we do with Pippins?" Ginger asked, feeling the heat of anger flushing her cheeks. "I'm hardly going to put him out to pasture."

"Don't be vulgar, my dear," Ambrosia said. "He can stay on staff with a modified role. Like that Marvin fellow."

Scout's face twisted, and Ginger gave him a firm look, clearly relaying that he'd better not open his mouth. Marvin Elliot was Scout's cousin, and after suffering a brain injury that summer, Ginger had offered him lodging at Hartigan House and a job doing light gardening under the watchful eye of Clement.

Ambrosia's snootiness was uncalled for, and at that moment, Ginger wanted to put *her* out to pasture. Indeed, she and Pippins were nearly the same age.

Basil rang the bell. "Anyone for a cup of strong coffee?"

Ginger smiled at her husband with appreciation. "I'd like one."

"As would I," Haley said. "Then I'm going to the

mortuary. Dr. Palmer has invited me to participate in the post-mortem as part of my practicum studies."

"Must we speak of such things at the breakfast table?" Ambrosia said. "I realise Americans are wild, but we appreciate polite restraint in England."

"I'm enjoying it on display right now," Haley said coyly.

Thankfully, Mrs. Beasley had anticipated a probable request for coffee, especially with Haley as a guest, and the pot quickly arrived. Family gatherings were nothing if not a spectacular display of decorum and mischief.

Ginger was eager for the breakfast to end so she could return to Pippins' side at the hospital. One shouldn't be left without visitors on Christmas Eve.

However, when Basil asked if she'd like to join him to speak to the witnesses at the bookshop—she often accompanied Basil, as an extension of her work at Lady Gold Investigations, on his cases as an unofficial consultant to the police—Ginger couldn't say no.

"They agreed to meet at the scene?" she asked. "That's rather unusual."

"Normally, I would've had them come to the Yard," Basil returned, "but I thought seeing the shop would help them remember what happened before the explosion." Basil pinched his lips. "And they didn't exactly agree. I directed my officers to go to the addresses they gave, unannounced."

"Yes," Ginger said, "being Christmas Eve, they might not be so accommodating otherwise."

"Precisely."

Ginger planted her hands on her hips. "I'll take the Crossley and meet you there. I plan to see Pippins immediately afterwards."

8

*A*s she parked near the front of the shop, Ginger tightened her blue-tweed winter coat around her and exited the motorcar. She pressed her chin into the wide fur collar as she braced herself against the cold and rain. Since the explosion happened at the back of the shop, the damage inside wasn't apparent from the street. A passer-by would simply think the bookshop had closed for Christmas if it weren't for the uniformed bobby standing on guard.

"Sir," the officer said as Basil approached, Ginger a step behind. "Mr. Jennings is inside with Cole."

"And Miss . . ." Basil checked his notepad. "Er, Glenda Gibbons?" Basil asked.

The officer shook his head. "She's proving to be a little harder to track down, but the officers are on it."

Ginger hoped the sales lady would be found. Crimes occurring over Christmas were more difficult to solve promptly, and as every investigator knew, time was of the essence when tracking a killer.

Mr. Douglas Jennings stood as Ginger and Basil entered the shop. He wore a black pin-striped suit with shiny black shoes. His hair was oiled, combed straight back off his forehead, and glistened under the electric ceiling lamp. He seemed nervous as to the protocol, holding his hand out to shake and then pulling it back.

"Thank you for meeting us, Mr. Jennings," Basil said. "This shouldn't take long, and then you can return to your business." He motioned to a stool by the sales desk. "Have a seat."

"Thank you, sir," the man said.

Basil gave the man a moment to relax before asking, "Can you lead us through the moments prior to the explosion?"

"Let's see. It's all just so shocking," Mr. Jennings started. "I can hardly wrap my mind around it."

"Do you recall where you were standing when it happened?" Ginger asked.

"Ah, yes." Mr. Jennings walked away from the

stool and took three paces to the centre of the room. "I generally stand around here, where any customer can seek me out from any corner of the shop."

Ginger tilted her head. "Did you see Miss Hartigan and Mr. Pippins enter?"

Mr. Jennings nodded vigorously. "I did. Not together, mind. The lady arrived first and the man about ten minutes later."

"What did Miss Hartigan do during those ten minutes?" Basil asked.

Mr. Jennings shrugged. "Browse the shelves, I suspect. I didn't pay her that much attention, to be honest. There were a lot of other customers in the shop as well, late Christmas shoppers."

"Did Miss Hartigan speak to any of the other customers?" Ginger asked.

"If she did, I never took note," Mr. Jennings answered. "But from my recollection, she did not. She seemed to pace the travel section, glancing at the back wall, but never removed a book. I remember thinking that was odd, but another customer needed my assistance, and I never gave it another thought. Until . . ."

"Until?" Basil prompted.

"Her companion joined her, that Mr. Pippins fellow." Mr. Jennings sniffed. "I hate to speak ill of the man since I know he was injured, but he seemed uneasy. Which made me uneasy, if you know what I mean."

Ginger prickled at the manager's insinuation. "I'm afraid I don't know what you mean, Mr. Jennings."

"It's just that it didn't seem like he'd come to shop. He went directly to the back of the shop to meet the lady—" He caught his breath. "I'm sorry, I've not seen a body since the war, and then it was always a fella's, wasn't it?"

"Your feelings are understandable," Basil said. "Take a moment, then, if you will, to recall what happened next."

"Yes, sir." Mr. Jennings straightened his tie as he inhaled. Having composed himself, he said, "The two of them seemed to be in an intense conversation, certainly not a light-hearted discussion of what books to purchase."

"Did you hear what they were saying?" Ginger asked.

"No, madam. They were too far away, but I did catch the elderly man's steely-blue eyes. He glanced at me, and I saw something in those eyes. Fear? Anger? Whatever it was, I didn't like it."

Ginger's hand went to the collar of her coat as

she tried to picture the scene. She'd never seen his eyes flash with any overt emotion in all her years of knowing Pips. Whatever it was that Florence had to say—whatever the reason they'd met here in the first place—must've been extremely upsetting to him.

"Do you have any idea how someone might have had an opportunity to set a bomb in your shop, Mr. Jennings?" Basil asked.

"I really don't know, sir. There are too many customers for me to keep an eye on them all, though . . ."

"Yes?" Basil prompted.

"A week ago, I had to sack a man. It was dreadfully bad timing with the Christmas rush. And now . . ." A muscle in his cheek twitched. "There's so much to do. Repairs, work to get the shop reopened as soon as possible. So many books lost."

"Indeed." Basil removed a small notepad and pencil from the pocket of his trench coat. "Mr. Jennings, what was the name of your former employee?"

"Crockett. William Crockett. And I hate to say it, but a key to the shop went missing."

"Thank you," Basil said as he jotted down the name and reference to the missing key. "You may go now. You won't mind if we call on you again in the future if we need to?"

Mr. Jennings nodded, his face an expression of relief. "Certainly, sir." With a nod to Ginger, he added, "Madam."

When he had gone, Ginger turned to Basil. "I believe he wished to thank us for shopping at Hatchards and stopped himself just in the nick of time."

Basil grinned as he checked his watch. "No Miss Gibbons?" he said to Constable Cole, who remained at the door.

"I believe that is her, sir."

She arrived with the winds, cheeks flushed, and her expression as hard as the slamming door. "It's Christmas Eve," she said. "Is nothing sacred?"

"We regret having to detain you in this manner, Miss Gibbons," Basil said with his usual charm. "Criminals can be rather inconsiderate in their timing, but I promise we'll be as quick as possible."

"I don't understand why I had to come back here," Miss Gibbons complained. "It's eerie."

"We thought it might jog your memory," Basil said.

Miss Gibbons gave Ginger a dismissive look as she opened the scarf around her neck. "Forgive me,

Chief Inspector; it's just all so alarming." She took a seat on the stool before it was offered, likely accustomed to being posted there when she worked. "I'll help in any way that I can."

"How long have you worked at Hatchards?" Ginger asked.

Londoners came with various accents, and one could usually pinpoint where a person was born and brought up. Miss Gibbons' accent was a little hard to read.

"I just moved to London last month," Miss Gibbons said, frowning.

Ginger leaned in. "Where did you live before you came to London?"

Annoyance flashed across the saleslady's face as her brown eyes settled on Basil. "What does this have to do with the explosion? I hardly had anything to do with it. You can ask anyone. I was working at the cash register the whole time."

"Perhaps nothing," Basil said, "but does it hurt to answer the question?"

Miss Gibbons pursed her lips before answering, "I worked in a bookshop in Watford. I've always wanted to move to London."

She shot Ginger an impertinent look as if to ask if Ginger was happy now.

She continued, "I was ringing up a customer, when all of a sudden, this dreadful noise filled the place, and bits of plaster fell from the ceiling from the rattling, and, well, it was horribly frightening. It reminded me of the Zeppelin bombing in the war."

"Mr. Jennings mentioned a missing key," Ginger said. "Do you know anything about that?"

Miss Gibbons shook her head. "No, madam."

"Did you happen to see anything out of the ordinary?" Basil asked. "Anything, in retrospect, that you'd consider unusual?"

"It was another busy day with people shopping for Christmas presents. I never really paid attention to anyone unless they were handing money over. Though . . ." Miss Gibbons worked her lips again, more vigorously this time.

"Miss Gibbons?" Basil prompted.

"I'm new to the city, so I can't say what's normal, but Mr. Jennings seemed on edge. Perhaps it was just the stress of the Christmas period, or you know, he was really distracted by that older couple in the back. I thought it strange but shrugged it off, you know? I forgot about it until now." She lifted both shoulders as she flicked a wrist. "Like you said, Chief Inspector. Coming back here did jog my memory."

9

Ginger had been warned by the nurse taking care of Pippins that he spoke in his sleep, sometimes rousing to wakefulness but not yet coherent.

"Will he know I'm here?" Ginger asked.

The nurse offered a soft, consolatory smile. "He'll know someone is here."

Basil had secured a small private room with a window and two plain wooden chairs for visitors. A small table beside the metal-pipe-framed bed had a water jug and a glass filled halfway.

Ginger's heart tightened at the thought of losing Pippins. Like everyone, Pippins wouldn't live forever, but she couldn't think of a life without him. Not yet.

Rubbing his cool hand between hers, she said, "Happy Christmas, Pippins. It's Christmas Eve, and the house feels . . . incomplete . . . without you."

Pippins' eyes flickered open to narrow slits, staring blankly. Surely, if he were looking for signs of Christmas, he wouldn't see them in this drab room! Ginger made a mental note to bring a cheery decoration the next time she came.

Pippins opened his mouth and spoke, his voice dry and raspy. "I don't mean to speak out of turn, miss."

"It's fine, Pippins," Ginger said. Perhaps he'd tell her something relevant to the explosion, even through his delirium. "You can speak freely. Did you see something at the bookshop?"

Pippins' long forehead buckled. "On the beach near the revolving tower. I saw you stepping out. With a gentleman. You looked very happy. The wind blowing in your hair."

Ginger let out a small breath. Pippins wouldn't be revealing a clue to Florence's death. However, Ginger believed Pippins was talking about Florence, so perhaps, in a roundabout way, he would.

"Do you know the man?" Ginger asked.

"I took the Model T. Just to pick up a few things for the kitchen. I left early, before the paper came;

otherwise, I would've stayed, miss. I would've warned you."

"Warned me of what, Pippins?" Ginger said, stepping into the role of Florence for his sake. "What happened?"

Pippins' hand, limp until this moment, tightened around Ginger's. His eyes opened wide, though unseeing, except for whatever reel might be playing in his mind. "The war, miss! Britain at War with Germany!"

"It's all right, Pippins," Ginger said soothingly. "The war is over. You're safe."

"*You're* not safe, miss. Your gentleman. He's in danger."

Pippins' head fell back as the tension in his body eased.

"Pippins?" Ginger said.

Whatever story Pippins was trying to relay had piqued her curiosity. If only he'd wake up, he could tell her what he knew about Florence and her gentleman friend. Who was he, exactly? Was he dangerous? Was he the one responsible for the bombing at the bookshop?

When it became clear that Pippins had fallen back into his comatose state, Ginger relinquished her vigil and trusted her butler's care to the hands of the saintlike nurses who were giving up their family time to take care of the ill and ailing. She had other responsibilities, including her Regent Street dress shop, Feathers & Flair. She wanted to call in to wish her manager, Madame Roux, and the rest of her staff a merry Christmas, ensure they received the gifts she had had delivered, and wrap up the last-minute shoppers.

Four years earlier, Ginger had opened the shop, almost on a whim, and was pleased with how well it was doing, especially with all the competition in London and other major European cities. Feathers & Flair had precisely that—extravagant and extraordinary designs housed in a tall limestone building with flair. Catching her reflection in the window glass—she wore a green fur-lined coat and a matching fur-trimmed hat and carried a sturdy umbrella against the pouring rain—Ginger was much like the customers often found in her shop.

Ginger had rented the ground floor and the first floor of the Regent Street building. Inside, the floors were tiled with glossy-white marble, the walls trimmed with cornice, and electric lights hung from above.

Millie, a tall, pretty girl and Constable Braxton's current sweetheart, modelled an original design created by Emma, Ginger's young and talented seamstress. The customer made happy noises of approval. "My daughter will adore it! It's the perfect dress for Christmas!"

Dorothy, who at first glance seemed a little out of place, came down the steps from the upper level where the factory designs were on display. A young lady and her beau walked behind her, and Ginger smiled at the blushing couple, guessing that the gentleman had just made an appropriate purchase as a gift for the lady.

Ginger was pleased with her success and attributed that to the shop's ability to attract and satisfy those with haute-couture tastes and those who wanted quick and easy access to the latest fashions.

Madame Roux, a refined lady who was intrinsically fashion-forward, strolled elegantly towards Ginger. Despite her years of living in London, her French accent remained intact, and quite by design, Ginger suspected.

"Madame Reed, 'ello, and Merry Christmas."

"Merry Christmas to you as well, Madame Roux," Ginger returned. "I trust the gifts I ordered came on time?"

"*Oui*, madame, they are unopened in the back. *Merci*. The girls and I are grateful."

Ginger had allowed that the presents—fine silk stockings—could be taken to their homes and placed under the Christmas tree.

The afternoon was busy with last-minute customers, some browsing and some making purchases, and time moved quickly. Soon the last customer had left the shop and Madame Roux locked the door behind them.

It was common for the girls to chit-chat whilst tidying up, and the subject quickly turned to the death at Hatchards.

"What happened, Mrs. Reed?" Millie asked as she removed an outfit from a floor mannequin. "Brian is so annoyingly tight-lipped."

Ginger was pleased to hear that Constable Braxton hadn't been tempted to relay police business to his sweetheart, Millie. "There was an explosion."

"I heard someone died," Emma said.

"That's true," Ginger said. "Sadly, it was a cousin of mine."

Madame Roux stilled at the open cash register, the cash now safely inside a bank bag. "Oh, Madame Reed, *je suis désolée*."

"And my poor butler was injured as well." Ginger hated to relay bad news on Christmas Eve, but the victims' names hadn't been withheld.

"Who would do such a terrible thing?" Dorothy said, having caught the conversation on her way down from the upper level. "And at Christmas!"

"A mad person," Millie replied. "That's who."

"I'm sorry to hear about your butler," Emma said. "That's Pippins, isn't it?"

Ginger nodded. "He's resting in hospital. We're hoping for a happy outcome."

"Will you still have your New Year's Eve party?" Millie asked. Pulling a face, she added, "I don't mean to be insensitive, but a girl has to plan ahead."

Madame Roux glared at Millie with disapproval as the other girls seemed to hold their breaths. Ginger had invited them all to celebrate the new year and could sense their impending disappointment.

"The party is still on," she said. "For now. You'll forgive me if I must cancel at the last minute, but I'm hopeful that won't be the case."

"We're so relieved," Dorothy said. "And wishing your Pippins a full and quick recovery."

It was Ginger's great wish as well.

10

When Basil returned to Scotland Yard, he was relieved to see Braxton on the premises. Basil had his pick of constables as a chief inspector, and Braxton had proven to be a competent assistant with a good sense of policing intuition.

"Braxton," Basil said. "Ring up the metro police station. Ask about a bloke by the name of William Crockett. He's a former bookshop employee who left under a cloud. I'd like to know if he's had any encounters with the law."

Braxton nodded. "Yes, sir."

Basil waited as the constable dialled a number on the candlestick phone and held the cone receiver to his ear. After informing the operator where he wanted to be connected, there was a pause before a man's voice came on the line.

"Yes, Will Crockett," Braxton confirmed. "Yes. Yes. Thank you, Constable."

Braxton hung up and stared at Basil. "It appears he's been in a few times, sir. Spent a night or two in the cells to sober up."

"Anything else?" Basil asked. "Petty theft?"

"There's something here about a complaint by a Mr. Douglas Jennings."

"That's the manager of the bookshop, the one who sacked Crockett."

Braxton nodded. "Yes, sir. It appears Mr. Jennings dropped the charges. He says Crockett pocketed cash from the cash register, but he couldn't prove it. Do you think this Crockett fellow might have something to do with the explosion?" Braxton asked. "Revenge, perhaps?"

Basil lifted a shoulder. "Who's to know, but it wouldn't hurt to ask the chap. Jot down the man's address, then come with me."

"Shall I get the key for a police motorcar, sir?" The fleet of Daimlers had self-starting buttons, but a key was needed to turn on the electrical circuit.

Basil adjusted his stance. "I think I'd rather take my own."

Braxton grabbed his helmet, then hurried to catch up with Basil as he headed for the door.

Despite his woollen trench coat and leather gloves, Basil didn't relish getting into an ice-cold motorcar, but such was the price of winter, and this one was proving to be particularly punishing. Once he had the Austin on the street, Basil shot his constable a sideways glance. "Do you have plans for Christmas, Constable?"

"Dinner with the family, sir. Tomorrow that is. Millie wants me to come to her place after work today to be with her family."

Millie was one of Ginger's girls at her dress shop. Basil knew Braxton and the mannequin were stepping out. "Is it serious, then?" he asked.

Braxton's lips pulled up. "I think so, sir."

"Ah, a ring under the tree, perhaps?"

Braxton's shoulders slumped. "No. But I think she might be hoping." He gave Basil a helpless look. "I think I might've messed things up, but I just couldn't bring myself to do it."

Basil kept his eyes on the road. Dealing with matters of the heart could be a minefield. "I suppose a man has to listen to his gut," he said.

Braxton turned in his seat. "Did you have any doubt, sir, with Mrs. Reed? Am I feeling what any normal man might feel?"

"Yes, regarding your second question," Basil said. "I believe what you're feeling is normal. But no, to your first question. I was quite certain Mrs. Reed was the lady for me." He smiled. "I was less certain she'd have me, though."

Relieved, Basil pulled his Austin to a stop in front of the address Braxton had given him. Whatever was to happen between his constable and sweetheart had nothing to do with him.

Will Crockett lived in a terraced house in the middle-class area of Bloomsbury. A landlady opened the front door and directed them to the second floor, where Crockett had a flat.

Basil had to knock several times, calling out the man's name, before the door opened. A set of bloodshot eyes stared back. Crockett wore pressed wide-legged trousers, cuffed at the ankles, and a striped collarless shirt. His attire had been fashionable a year or two earlier and had a thin and worn appearance.

"I'm not blasted buying."

"And we're not selling, Mr. Crockett," Basil said. He flashed his identification card. "I'm Chief

Inspector Basil Reed, and this is Constable Braxton. We'd like a few minutes of your time."

"Ah, if this is about that deuced Jennings, it was just a damned misunderstanding."

"All the same, we'd like to ask you a few questions."

"Bloody hell, then. Come in."

Crockett flung the door open, and as Basil led the way inside, he was accosted by unpleasant smells —a mix of stale cigarette smoke, cheap alcohol, and unwashed skin.

"You can sit down if you like," Crockett said, "but don't expect no refreshments."

The room consisted of well-made furniture, looking tired with extended neglect.

"We can stand," Basil said. "We don't intend to take up much of your time."

"Suit yourselves," Crockett said as he collapsed into a well-worn armchair. He flicked a wrist. "Ask away."

"The manager of Hatchards claims that you helped yourself from the till, ostensibly to support your, er . . ." Basil let his gaze drift over an array of empty bottles laying around before finishing with, "fondness for drink."

"That is a lie," Crockett returned glibly. "I didn't need to steal from the blasted till because I had a job and could pay for my pleasures. At least until he sacked me."

"Did you ever go back to the bookshop?" Basil asked.

Crockett huffed. "Why would I?"

"How about after-hours? Mr. Jennings claims a key to the front door went missing."

"It wasn't me," Crockett said with indignation. "I slapped the key on the counter. Ask that shrew, Miss Gibbons."

Basil glanced at Braxton, ensuring the constable had noted that down in his notepad. Then he said, "Miss Gibbons claims she never saw a key."

"Blasted liar." Crockett sniffed. "I don't know what that lot has against me. I'm an educated man with years of experience working in bookshops."

Crockett lifted a shaky hand. Half his middle finger and both his ring and little fingers were missing. Basil tried to imagine someone rigging a bomb in the alcove behind a bookshelf with that handicap. Not impossible, but difficult.

"Bloody war," Crockett explained, then grinned crookedly. "At least I have one good hand. All I need to lift a bottle."

"Thank you, Mr. Crockett." Basil returned his hat to his head. "That will do for now. Happy Christmas."

Crockett snorted. "Bah. Humbug."

11

The evening of Christmas Eve was one of Ginger's favourite times of the year. Lizzie and Grace had done a marvellous job of decorating each room with garlands of holly and mistletoe —Clement assisting when a ladder was required for hard-to-reach areas. Hartigan House enjoyed the modern convenience of electricity, and strands of fairy lights brought a sense of otherworldliness to the house. The drawing room housed the Christmas tree, a large and broad feather tree with plenty of room for decorations—colourful glass balls, tinsel, and candles, which would be lit during Basil's story time. Ginger loved the tradition where Basil read delightful Christmas tales, including the Christmas story from *The Bible* in the book of Luke.

All the family was present: Ambrosia, Felicia and Charles, Ginger and Basil, and the children, with Haley rounding out the crew. The staff—Mrs. Beasley, Clement, Lizzie and Grace, Nanny Green, and Ambrosia's maid Langley—were having their own celebration in the kitchen with mulled wine and mince pies. Scout's cousin Marvin, who had recently moved into a room above the garage, had joined them. Only poor Pippins was missing from the group, still resting in his hospital room.

"The photographer should be here soon," Ginger said. Stepping toward the long windows and pushing apart the light rose-coloured curtains, she frowned at the pouring rain, barely able to make out the street through dramatic weather.

Basil stepped in beside her. "The poor bloke will ruin his equipment."

"Oh mercy," Ginger said. "I suppose I should let the man know we can book the session for another day. Only, I was so hoping for a Christmas memory."

Haley chirped up, "I could take the photograph. You have a camera in the house, right?"

"I do." Ginger considered her friend's offer. "And I have a dark room at the office of Lady Gold Investigations." She smiled. "If you don't mind, Haley."

"Of course not."

Ginger rang for Lizzie to cancel the photographer.

Lizzie offered a small curtsey and said, "A message just arrived, madam. The photographer sends his regrets, but the weather is too prohibitive."

"Very well," Ginger said. "Is everything all right in the kitchen?" She wanted her staff to have a relaxing Christmas Eve, even though they had to wait on the family.

Lizzie smiled. "Quite, madam. Mrs. Beasley has outdone herself this year with the cooking and baking. There's plenty for us all."

Ginger dismissed her maid, then announced to the room. "Please excuse me whilst I round up my camera. Haley has kindly offered to take our family photographs in lieu of the photographer who has cancelled due to the storm raging outside.

Sitting on the settee with little Rosa on her lap, Felicia cooed at the child happily. "Oh no. The weather is too bad. Uncle Charles and I might have to stay the night in your crib. You don't mind, little princess, do you?"

Rosa, cheeks red from the warmth given off by the roaring fire in the stone fireplace, laughed at

Felicia as if she understood the joke behind the statement's absurdity.

"Ambrosia seems a little more morose than usual," Ginger said to Basil. "Why don't you see if you can cheer her up?"

Basil cocked a brow. "Shall I have Scout play a tune on the grand piano?"

Ginger stared back at her husband in horror. As much as she loved Scout and allowed him every opportunity to try new things, musical ability didn't come easily to the lad. "Why don't you offer her a drink instead," she said. "I believe Clement ensured that the drinks trolley was fully stocked."

Soon, Ginger and Haley had the camera equipment set up, and Ginger, with some effort positioned everyone in place, with herself, Basil, and the children in the centre. Haley pointed Ginger's camera, a French 35 mm Furet, at the group. "Everyone, smile."

Ambrosia blustered. "Smile?"

"Smiling together makes us all look as if we're happy to be doing this," Ginger replied.

"I find it manipulative," Ambrosia returned, affronted.

Thankfully, the affair didn't take all that long, and they regrouped in a semicircle around the fireplace, snacking on an array of Christmas treats and drinking hot chocolate spiked with brandy.

Ginger opened the baby grand and played a medley of Christmas carols, and before long, the evening passed, and it was time for Rosa to go to bed. She had fallen asleep in Felicia's arms, and Felicia reluctantly handed the toddler over to Nanny Green.

Eventually, Ambrosia announced she'd reached the end of her day, and Scout headed up shortly after her.

"I'm reading a good book," he announced. His eyes darted to the pile of gifts under the tree. "I'll be sure to arise early tomorrow morning."

"Don't forget there's church afterwards, darling," Ginger said.

"I suppose we should wander home as well," Charles said, rising. "Even though we're just across the street, it might take a while to push through this weather."

As if on cue, the wind howled through the window.

"Oh, please stay for another round of mulled wine," Ginger said. "Perhaps the weather will calm down in an hour or so."

Felicia and Charles accepted the invitation, and

an extra log was placed on the fire, its flames flickering and wood snapping in a delightfully cosy manner.

Ginger snuggled into Basil's side, curling up with Boss, who'd remained behind. Her Boston terrier had become Scout's good companion these last years, but his loyalty and devotion remained with Ginger. She patted his head, and he nudged her fondly in return.

"Happy Christmas, Boss," she said.

At nine years old, Boss wasn't a puppy anymore and had slowed down a lot lately. He hesitated a little at the bottom of the staircase before scampering up and spent more time napping. The black patch of his body showed signs of greying. Ginger couldn't picture a time without the little fellow and forced her mind to other happier thoughts. Christmas Eve had been a delightful time with her family, and bright-eyed Rosa brought everyone the extra cheer needed.

If only Pippins were well and with them.

"We'll celebrate again," Basil said, "when he's home."

Ginger stared at Basil, surprised at his intuitiveness. "When did you become a mind reader?"

Basil smirked. "Today. I asked Father Christmas to let me peek into my beautiful wife's intriguing mind."

Charles slapped his lap. "I knew I should've asked for that." He reached for Felicia's hand, his eyes forming wrinkles at the corners as he smiled. "You'll forgive me, darling, if, for another year, I fail to read your mind?"

Felicia laughed, her delicate chin jutting upwards. "If you forgive me for not reading yours."

Felicia and Charles sat closely on the other settee, leaving Haley solo on a wingback chair. Ginger hoped her friend would find love one day, as she and Felicia had. Still, for now, Haley seemed sincerely contented to be single in this world, her driving desire to become a doctor—truly a grand design considering men dominated science and medicine. If anyone had the drive to take on prejudice and outdated protocol, it was Haley Higgins.

"You haven't had a chance to relay your visit today," Haley said. "How is Pippins doing?"

Ginger straightened out her stocking-covered legs, stretching them as she pointed her patent-leather, double-buckle shoes.

"It's hard to say. Both times I've visited, he's been incoherent. It's as if he's aware someone's in the room and desperately wants to rouse himself awake."

"Does he speak at all?" Charles asked.

"Yes," Ginger said, "and I can understand what

he says, though it doesn't make sense. I believe he thinks I'm Florence Hartigan." Ginger narrowed her eyes. "I think he's trying to warn her."

Felicia gasped, her hand reaching for the rope of pearls around her neck. "Poor thing. He's too late."

"What did he say, exactly?" Haley asked. "Did he mention the hand bomb?"

Ginger shook her head. "No, nothing like that. He speaks like he's back when he worked for cousin Florence. He mentioned a gentleman."

Basil crossed his legs as he considered Ginger's words. "Was he warning Miss Hartigan about him?"

"I think so," Ginger said. "He said cousin Florence wasn't safe and the man she'd been stepping out with was a danger."

"A mystery man," Felicia said. "What a good idea. I need a twist for the book I'm working on." Felicia had enjoyed a little success as a published mystery writer, though she wrote under the pen name Frank Gold. "My editor says my books on the shelves at Hatchards were spared, though they may smell a little smoky."

Haley lifted a shoulder. "Too bad we can't find out who this gentleman was."

"If there was such a thing," Basil said. "The poor fellow might just be talking whilst dreaming."

"When exactly would this encounter have happened?" Charles asked. He held Ginger's gaze for a moment before letting it fall away.

Ginger and Charles shared a secret, one neither of their spouses knew about—even though Ginger knew that Basil had his suspicions. Both she and Charles had spent time in the British secret service. Ginger gave up her official involvement once the Great War had ended, but Charles continued to serve under the guise of being busy with the House of Lords. This knowledge was an understanding between them but never spoken unless life or limb depended on it. They had the Official Secrets Act to thank for that.

Ginger pushed a short lock of red hair behind her ear as she leaned forward. "It's my under-standing that Pippins moved to Great Yarmouth in 1914, shortly after the assassination of Archduke Franz Ferdinand. Hartigan House had been shut at the end of 1913 and stayed that way for ten years."

"We're looking at a decade-long period," Charles returned. "Searching for a man who may not exist would be like looking for the proverbial needle in the haystack. Though—" The firelight cast flicking light across Charles' face as he paused.

Basil raised a brow as he stared at Charles from across the room. "Though, old chap?"

Charles shifted in his seat as his expression struggled with indecision. "I have contacts in Great Yarmouth. From the old days, old boy. Perhaps someone might know. A mutual friend of Miss Hartigan's?"

"How intriguing," Felicia said after a sip of mulled wine. "But you may be right, dear. Britain isn't huge. Someone must know something."

"Did Pippins happen to say anything else that might be of use?" Haley asked.

"Yes," Ginger said. "He announced the beginning of the war as if it had just become known."

"That may narrow the window of time in which to identify the man," Basil said.

"The summer of fourteen," Ginger said. "Hopefully, Charles, that will be of some help."

Charles raised his nearly empty glass. "One can hope." He shot what remained of his mulled wine down his throat, then turned to Felicia. "Well, dear? Shall we call it a night?"

"Yes, we shall." Felicia offered her hand to Charles, and he helped her to her feet. The rest of them rose as well, extending quick embraces and wishes of happy Christmas.

"If you don't mind," Haley said, "I'll head off to bed now."

"Reading to do?" Ginger asked with a grin.

Haley chuckled. "You know me too well, old friend."

Ginger lingered behind as Basil poked at the dying coals in the fire, spreading them to extinguish any remaining flames. The room was in disarray, but the maids would rise early to tidy up before the Christmas morning festivities began. Basil returned, took Ginger's hand, and led her out of the room, stopping only to kiss her under the mistletoe that hung over the doorway.

"I do believe you owe me a kiss, Mrs. Reed," he said as he embraced her.

"Or is it you who owes me?" Ginger returned playfully.

Basil ducked his chin. "I'll meet you halfway."

Ginger brushed her lips against his. "As you always do, love."

12

Christmas day began early the next morning with presents exchanged and cups of coffee drunk. A special breakfast of smoked salmon and scrambled eggs, along with the traditional glass of champagne, awaited the family in the morning room, then there was a frantic rush to prepare for church. Ambrosia, Felicia and Charles attended one of the parish churches in South Kensington whilst Ginger and Basil drove to London, where St. George's Church was located. Ginger's dear friends Reverend Oliver Hill and his wife, Matilda, were why the Reeds attended the little stone church. In fact, Ginger and Oliver had formed a friendship before either was married and together had started the Child Wellness Project to help street children with meals and other means of support.

The church, an eighteenth-century structure built with limestone, had a tall square tower over the entrance. Stained glass lined the exterior walls of the nave, culminating in a masterful stained-glass wall behind the pulpit depicting Jesus and the saints.

The precipitation had prevented many from attending the service, which said volumes about the nastiness of the weather, that it would keep people from church on Christmas morning. The Reed clan took up an entire row, with Ginger and Basil seated together, Scout next to Basil and Haley, and Nanny Green with Rosa next to Ginger.

Oliver stood at the pulpit, a friendly smile of welcome on a long face sprinkled with freckles. His red hair was oiled into submission, an effort that barely erased the child within the man. Wearing a white surplice and a long purple stole embroidered with the Christmas star, he began, "Glory to God in the highest . . ."

After the service, he greeted Ginger warmly. "Happy Christmas, Ginger." He shook her hand vigorously, then offered a handshake to Basil. "Mr. Reed." To Haley, he said, "Miss Higgins! What a delight to see you again. You must say hello to

Matilda. She has a special place in her heart for you, as you know."

Ginger and Haley had helped Matilda through a distressing time, and Haley's medical knowledge had saved the woman's life.

"Of course, Reverend," Haley said. "I wouldn't miss a chance to greet your lovely wife again."

"Very good," Reverend Hill said, then turned to Scout. "Look how tall you've got, young man. I hear you're doing well at your new boarding school. One that specialises in equines?"

"Yes, sir," Scout said. "I intend to work with horses and hope to be a jockey one day."

Oliver patted Scout on the back. "And a fine one you'll be, I'm sure."

Ginger and Haley left Oliver to go and talk to Matilda. Both Ginger and Matilda had young daughters in their arms. After exchanging greetings, Matilda commented, "I rarely see you with little Rosa. She's such a pretty little thing."

While Ginger had the advantage of engaging a nanny, Matilda had to care for her child on her own, a task she didn't seem to mind. Still, Ginger felt the need to defend herself. "I'm with her a lot whilst at home, though I don't take her out and about as much."

"I meant no offence," Matilda said. She shifted little Margaret to her other hip and took a moment to pat the base of her bobbed hair. "We should have tea sometime in the new year. Let the girls play together."

Ginger smiled. "I'd like that."

Leaving Haley to continue chatting—the two seemed to have a more natural connection—Ginger sought Basil and Scout. Basil was engaged in conversation with a fellow officer who also went to St. George's. Ginger was on her way to them when her path crossed once again with Oliver.

"Oliver," she said, shifting Rosa on her hip, "I'm worried about the street children. The news reports on the wireless are predicting a dreadful storm."

For the first time, Oliver's countenance clouded. "I've heard that too. As you know, we sponsor a Christmas dinner for them and anyone else on the street who needs food and warmth. The church hall will be made up for those who need shelter from the cold. We have plenty of camp beds and blankets from the war years when the church was used as a place for soldiers to convalesce."

Rosa fussed, and Nanny Green appeared at Ginger's side. "Would you like me to take her, madam?"

"Thank you," Ginger said, handing Rosa over.

Nanny Green expertly soothed Rosa and sat with her in a pew as she waited.

"I'm pleased to hear that care is being offered," Ginger said, turning back to Oliver.

Oliver grinned. "Much of it's due to your generosity, Ginger. Thank you again for your handsome year-end donation."

Ginger waved a gloved hand. "It's nothing. I'm happy I can help."

Oliver's red brows lifted. "I've just recalled the difficulties your butler has been enduring. Forgive my relapse. How is the old fellow faring?"

"He's improving steadily," Ginger said. "I'm hoping to bring him home soon. In fact, I plan to head to the hospital from here to wish him a happy Christmas."

Another congregant called Oliver away, and Ginger rejoined Basil, relaying her desire. "I'd like to call at the hospital to see Pippins. Perhaps Haley and I can go if you don't mind returning home with Nanny Green and the children."

"I'll see if I can wave down a taxicab," Basil said.

Haley was happy to return to the hospital with Ginger, and thankfully, Basil waved down a taxicab, though, despite his umbrella, he returned to the church vestibule soaking wet.

"Oh, Basil," Ginger said, grinning. "You're drenched."

Basil grinned back. "What a man won't do for love." He gave her a quick kiss on the cheek. "Don't be long. The weather is only going to get worse."

Ginger and Haley climbed into the taxicab with instructions to be taken to St. Bartholomew's Hospital.

"Yes, madam," the man said. He levelled out his hat. "I hope you won't mind if we drive slowly. The weather's rather on the dodgy side."

The rain snapped off the windscreen, and even though the wipers worked hard, visibility through the murky window was most definitely impaired. Haley held the handgrip in much the same way she did when Ginger was driving in good weather. Ginger smirked, thinking that some people just aren't comfortable in motorised vehicles.

Arriving at the hospital after what felt like an insufferably slow journey, Ginger paid the driver, asking him to retrieve them in an hour. The driver tipped his hat, promising that he would.

Ginger and Haley made their way to Pippins' room found a nurse attending to him. His long body was stretched out under a couple of blankets, and a nightcap had been placed on his head, making him look like a tall, sleepy elf.

"How is he?" Ginger asked.

"His pulse is still weak but getting stronger," the nurse said as she released his wrist. She then added with a smile, "Your friend is quite a fighter."

Ginger's heart warmed. "He's one of the most determined fellows I know."

"He's been a bit restless," the nurse continued. "Moaning in his sleep. He's calmer now but do let me know if he appears troubled or uncomfortable, and I'll call the doctor."

"Thank you, nurse," Ginger said.

There were two chairs in the room, and Ginger and Haley each took one, hanging their coats on the back before sitting.

Ginger reached for Pippins' hand. "Hello, Pips," she said softly. To Haley, she added, "His hands are warmer, and there's more colour in his cheeks."

"That's a good sign," Haley said. "Though, I imagine things will have to change."

"What do you mean?"

"He's an elderly man, Ginger. You don't think he can return to his butler duties, do you? You'll have to hire someone new."

Ginger sighed. "I know that you're right, of course. It's just hard to imagine Hartigan House with someone else at the helm. He'll always be family, and he'll always have a place with us."

"It'll be fine, I'm sure," Haley said. "He'll keep the new butler in line."

Ginger didn't relish going through the interview process. Good butlers were hard to find. The younger lot didn't always understand the seriousness of the position, and the older ones were often set in their ways, having been trained by someone else. Alas. But it was a problem for another time.

"I'll not think of it until next year," she said lightly, knowing the old joke with the following year only a week away.

Ginger glanced about, taking in the thick tinsel streaming in loops along the wall, with Christmas cards hanging from them. "At least someone went to the trouble of trying to add a bit of cheer."

Pippins emitted a soft moan.

"Pippins?" Ginger said.

Pippins twitched under his covers, making another muffled sound.

"Is he trying to speak?" Ginger asked.

"Perhaps," Haley said, "or he might be dreaming."

Ginger squeezed Pippins' bony hand. "Pippins? It's Mrs. Reed and Miss Higgins. We've come to wish you a happy Christmas."

Pippins' eyelids flickered, his blue eyes opening but looking past her. He opened his dry lips, struggling to speak.

"Pippins?" Ginger said. "What is it?"

With a raspy voice, he said, "What's behind the wall?"

Ginger shared a look with Haley, who said, "What wall?"

Casting a glance over her shoulder, Ginger doubted Pippins meant the wall of his hospital room. "I don't know. When I was here last, he thought I was cousin Florence."

"I wonder if he's fallen back in time in his mind," Haley said. "I've read about the phenomenon in patients who've experienced trauma."

Ginger lifted a shoulder. "I don't know. The last person he was with before the explosion was cousin Florence. Perhaps he simply remembers his time working for her."

"He looks upset," Haley said. "Was it an unpleasant time?"

Ginger regarded her friend. "Perhaps it was. He worked for her during the war years, which was a difficult time for everyone, of course." Regretfully she added, "You know, I never asked him about his time away from Hartigan House. I just assumed those waiting for the war to end didn't suffer as much as those who fought."

Pippins coughed, and Ginger reached for the glass of water on the table. "Here, Pips, have a drink." Ginger lifted her butler's head, more conscious than ever of his frailty, and carefully helped him as he took a small drink of water. She no longer worried that he'd no longer be fit to serve as her butler. She worried now that he might never leave this hospital.

Haley said, as if reading Ginger's mind, "He'll be all right. Maybe we should go and let him rest." She checked her wristwatch, then said, "Our hour is almost up."

"Yes, we should go," Ginger agreed. "I think Pips can sense that we're here, and he may not settle until we leave."

Ginger gathered her handbag, and with a final look out of the window, she gasped at the large snowflakes slowly falling to the ground below.

*a*s Miss Hartigan's butler, it is my duty to manage the entire household, especially in these tumultuous times. The war has created shortages everywhere, and it just won't do that the numbers aren't adding up.

I wrestle with the accounting, checking the supplies, and factoring in the number residing at The Willows. Besides myself, there's the cook, Mrs. Underhill; the housemaid, Penny; the gardener, Finch, who, like me, is too old to enlist; and Miss Hartigan. With only five to account for, it should be easy to manage what's needed and what's coming in.

Yet, the supplies are short. I let out a long, hard breath. It can only mean one thing: there is a thief amongst us. It behoves me to get to the bottom of this horrid affair before delivering word of it to Miss Hartigan.

I begin with Mrs. Underhill, who eyes me coolly when I approach her in the kitchen.

"As you can see, Mr. Pippins," she says, "I'm rather busy, doing my best with very little leading up to Christmas."

"As I've said, Mrs. Underhill, Miss Hartigan isn't expecting much for Christmas this year. The butcher has promised us a goose."

It's a promise I hope the man will keep, though I know I'm not the only one asking. Now, with us nearing the end of 1915, everything, including meat, is being tinned or dried and shipped to the men in the field. I can only imagine the Christmas those lads have to look forward to. "We'll make do with whatever we have," I add.

While weighing a portion of flour, Mrs. Underhill lifts the bag and wrinkles her nose at its lack of weight. "We're about to run out, Mr. Pippins."

"Thank you for mentioning that," I say, though I'm quite aware of the matter. "I have our name down for when another delivery arrives at the shop."

Mrs. Underhill stills and stares at me with tired eyes, the bluish circles growing deeper as the months of struggle continue to pass. "Is there something you need from me?"

"I have a rather delicate enquiry, I'm afraid."

"Oh?"

"In your opinion, have we been going through our food and drink supplies quicker than usual?"

Her cheeks flush at the question, and she turns away. "I don't think so. And I must insist that you leave the affairs of the kitchen to me."

"Of course," I add quickly. "It's just that I can't help noticing the state of the pantry."

"If the goose comes in as you hope, Mr. Pippins," Mrs. Underhill answers tersely, "then all will be well."

I clasp my hands behind my back and leave the housekeeper to her task. On my way out, I pass Penny. She's as skinny as a skeleton. I can hardly fault her if she sneaks extra food because she is starving, but the amount missing can hardly be attributed to one thin girl.

If I accept that the staff is not taking the food, and I do, then it leaves only two options: a burglar makes regular stops for food, or Miss Hartigan herself is consuming the extra food. Since the mistress hasn't put on weight and looks thinner than ever, it must be *a burglar. I will lock every door and window in the evenings from now on.*

Slipping into my overcoat, I wrap a muffler around my neck and head outside for a brisk walk, thinking a good gulp of sea air will do me good. The area hasn't had a white Christmas in ages, and this one isn't expected to be any different. Only rain, which thankfully has subsided for a few hours. I search for Finch, finding him sweeping mud off the walkway.

"Finch, old man," I say as I approach. He's wearing rubber boots and a mackintosh, both glossy with rain. His rather prominent nose is red from the cold.

"Good day, Pippins," Finch says with a ready smile. "Out for a walk in the damp, eh?"

"Need to clear my head," I say. "Look, have you seen any strangers milling about? Blokes who have no business in these parts?"

Finch frowns as he gives his head a quick shake. "Can't say I have. Is there a problem?"

"Probably not," I say. "These days, one can't be too careful. Hard times can drive good folks to do things they normally wouldn't."

Finch agrees. "Indeed, and I fear times will get more difficult yet."

"Sadly," I say, then let Finch return to his work. I turn towards the house, and after a few steps, I pause to study the structure. It could use paint, but that will have to wait until after the blasted war ends. A couple of ceramic roof tiles have come loose, an easy fix for Finch, assuming he's steady on a ladder. I'm about to head back to the man to point this out when I realise something.

Since arriving a year and a half ago, I've spent nearly all my time inside The Willows and have become quite well acquainted with the rooms. Yet, as I study the length of the house's exterior, it doesn't feel right. Being a fairly tall man, I have a stride of about three feet. I pace the length of the house, counting twenty-five paces or about seventy-five feet.

And what of those windows on the end? They are darkened as if covered in heavy drapery and dusty in a way that causes me to fault Penny.

With my hands behind my back, I return to the servants' entrance, then head to the corridor upstairs.

Starting at the most southward end, an unused bedroom, I count my strides until I'm at the end of the corridor. There are doors on either side leading to bedrooms, but on the wall at the end hangs a large tapestry depicting two unicorns. When Miss Hartigan had given me the first tour of the house, she'd mentioned that it had been made in Belgium and was expensive. Without touching it, I can tell it's made from high-quality material and is very thick.

I'm standing precisely sixty-eight paces from the south wall of the house. I pace it off three times to make sure.

The result is clear: even after considering the thickness of the walls, there is about eighteen feet of space behind that wall.

14

The snowfall continued throughout the night, painting London in a rare wash of white. Boxing Day was a bank holiday, so most people holed up in their houses and drank tea in front of coal fires. Children delighted themselves in frosty games of snowball fights or building snowmen who, coming from the result of a freak British snowstorm, were unlikely to have long lives.

Those working in service weren't enjoying the peace of sound-deadening snow or slowing physical activity, as it was their one day off over Christmas. Their dreams of leaving the family for which they worked and gaining precious time with their own families, were being dashed.

Ginger found Lizzie sobbing in the corridor. "I'm

sorry, madam, it's just that my mama has a goose, and all my brothers and sisters will be there. Grace is beside herself as well."

As well as Pippins, Mrs. Beasley and Clement lived at Hartigan House whilst the maids often spent the night; they went home to their families when they could. The elder servants were happy just to put their feet up and rest in solitude, perhaps with a good book or listening to the wireless Ginger had provided for them.

Ginger patted Lizzie on the shoulder. "Cheer up. I'm sure we can find a way to get you and Grace to your families."

Lizzie sniffed, her eyes widening with hope. "How can we, madam? The buses aren't running, and the pavement is too difficult to walk along to get to the underground."

Ginger's mind worked, quickly settling on a memory that might provide a solution. "How is your balance, Lizzie?"

Lizzie flashed a quizzical look. "Good enough, I suppose."

"Find Grace, and once the two of you are dressed warmly, meet me out at the garage."

Ginger found the warm winter clothes she had worn skiing and, after removing her skirt, adorned a pair of boys' long johns. Basil happened to be walking through the entrance hall as she descended the curved staircase looking like one heading for the slopes. Basil jerked at the sight of her.

"Pray tell, what are you up to now?"

"Lizzie and Grace are distraught about the snow keeping them from the Christmas celebrations they had planned with their families. I recalled that the cross-country skis we brought back from France are stored in the garage. I intend to retrieve them for the maids."

"You're proposing that they ski home?" Basil said as Ginger reached him. "Through the streets of London?"

Ginger adjusted her fur hat. "Why not?"

When Ginger reached the back garden, she found Scout, bundled up with a wool muffler and mittens, playing in the snow with Boss. Scout rolled the snow into three balls—one large, one medium, and one small—as Boss barked his excitement. Ginger laughed at the scene.

"I'm making a snowman," Scout said. "Mrs. Beasley even had an old carrot she said I could use for the nose."

"This reminds me of Boston!" Ginger said. "Only there, no one was excited about a snow day."

Scout's cheeks were red from the cold or the exertion; Ginger wasn't sure which.

"I love the snow!" Scout said. "How lucky for those who get it all winter long." As if noticing Ginger's outfit for the first time, he added, "What are you up to?"

"Lizzie and Grace need to borrow our cross-country skis."

Scout wrinkled his nose. "We have cross-country skis?"

"From a long time ago. I hope they're still stored in the garage. Come along and help."

Ginger led the way to the garage and opened the door. Clement had shovelled the snow that morning, even though there was no way anyone would be driving a motorcar off the premises.

The garage was wide enough to fit two vehicles, and they had to shuffle around the Crossley and Austin parked inside.

Ginger tilted her head to look up. "There, in the rafters. Do you see them?"

Scout nodded, then located a ladder leaning against the back wall. "I can get them down for you, Mum."

By the time Scout had extracted two pairs of

wooden skis from the rafters, Lizzie and Grace had arrived at the garage.

"What an exciting idea!" Lizzie gushed.

Grace wasn't as confident. "Won't we sink in the snow?"

"Not at all," Ginger said. "You'll glide over the top."

Lizzie turned out to be a natural and demonstrated the technique on the snow in the back garden. "It's like skating, Grace," she said.

Grace frowned. "I've never skated."

It took the maid a few attempts and a couple of discouraging falls in the snow before she found her rhythm. Scout was quick to assist when Grace needed help getting back on her feet, and it warmed Ginger's heart to see him acting as a gentleman, despite their class differences.

After promising to be back as soon as they could the next day, the two maids disappeared down the back alley.

Scout clapped his mitts together to release a few clumps of snow. "I'm going to try skiing when they get back."

"Until then," Ginger started, "your poor snowman is still lying in pieces."

"Righto," Scout said, sounding like Basil. She couldn't help but smile.

AFTER LOUNGING about on Boxing Day, Basil was eager to get back to the Yard the next morning and focus on the case. It'd been four days since the blast at Hatchards, and the timing over Christmas had hindered a proper investigation, a fact that made Basil's chest tighten with aggravation. The more time that went by without finding the killer, the less likely they were to do so. He hoped he'd get a small break in the case soon. He owed it to Ginger and Pippins to find out who had committed this horrible crime and to do so quickly.

The weather hadn't improved overnight. Lizzie had been the first to return with skis, and Basil immediately claimed them. Basil guessed his journey would be at least three miles and that it would take him a good hour to reach his destination. At least he could take a shortcut through St. James' Park. By the time he reached Scotland Yard, Basil had broken into a sweat and developed a demanding thirst which he was quick to relieve when he arrived.

It was a skeleton crew at the Yard, and Basil realised with a start he hardly recognised anyone.

The poor blokes who had to work despite the extreme weather were the constables, those without seniority. They didn't seem to have the same problem with him. Each stared back with eyes showing surprise that he'd shown up, then in turn, pronouncing hope that the Chief Inspector had a nice Christmas.

"I did, thank you, and I hope you did too," Basil returned. "Is there any news to report?"

"No, sir," an officer behind the counter said. "Perhaps the criminal element is taking time to celebrate as well."

"Or sleep one off," another chided. Seeing Basil's unsmiling face, he added, "Shall I get you a cup of tea, sir?"

Basil nodded. "That would be splendid, thank you."

His office at the Yard was unspectacular, barely half the size of the garage at Hartigan House, but it suited Basil just fine. He needed nothing larger than what would accommodate his desk, a couple of chairs, and a filing cabinet.

Basil closed the door, settled into his office chair, opened a desk drawer, and removed a file. In it was everything he knew about the case already.

He opened it on the top of his desk as a knock

was followed by the delivery of his tea. He thanked the officer, then said, "Close the door behind you, please."

Alone again, Basil blew on his tea before sipping, then flipped through the file which contained his initial report from the day of the blast, statements from the clerk and saleslady at Hatchards, and a preliminary report from Dr. Palmer at the mortuary.

The police photographs had been developed and delivered, and Basil gave each one a good look and sighed when he reached the last one. Nothing shed light on who had been responsible for the blast.

Mr. Jennings and Miss Gibbons' statements were straightforward, and if there was anything in there of import, Basil wasn't seeing it now. The report from Dr. Palmer was preliminary since the autopsy was scheduled to be performed the next day. Florence Hartigan had died due to injuries incurred by her closeness to the blast; the details of the exact cause of death were to come with the pathology report.

Basil let out another long breath. The papers were all over the extraordinary event with important headlines like "A Blast of a Christmas" and "Blasted Books Ruin Shoppers' Day." The write-ups themselves were useless as the "journalists" were looking to sell papers, not to relay the actual news, and naturally, the writers knew less than Basil did himself.

Retrieving a notepad and pencil from the top drawer, he jotted down notes from Ginger's visits to Pippins. Though the man was mentally incapacitated at the moment, he was their most important witness. At the top, he scribbled "Mystery Man". Was this person who Pippins had mentioned real or imaginary? An attack such as this one was clearly passionate, which would make it personal. Had Florence Hartigan spurned a lover? Was this revenge?

What kind of man would resort to riddles and elaborate schemes to kill a woman he once loved? Certainly, there were easier ways to dispatch someone.

His office door blew open. At first, Basil thought it was a young officer with another offer of tea, but to his surprise, the burly form of his superior officer stood in the doorway.

"Superintendent Morris," Basil said as he stood. "I hope you had a good Christmas."

Morris grunted.

"I'm surprised to see you here," Basil said, though pointing out that Morris had a family at home *would* be rather hypocritical.

"You're here," Morris returned, obviously thinking the same. He waved a thick palm. "Sit down."

Basil did as instructed, straightening his tie to defuse his nerves. Morris rarely sat Basil down to announce good news. "Sir?" he prompted.

"This bombing at the bookshop." Morris clicked his tongue. "A nasty affair."

"Indeed, sir."

"I understand your wife's cousin was killed and her butler injured."

Basil sighed. He knew now where this was going. "This won't affect my ability to investigate, sir."

"It's a clear conflict of interest," Morris returned. "I want West to take over. Look, Reed, you're not the only investigator at the Yard worth his weight. Let another man do this one."

"I'm not a direct family member of the victim; I've never even met her."

"But the butler—"

"He's not talking right now, but when he does, he's more likely to open up to me than a stranger. Don't forget he's in his seventies and set in his ways."

"Reed . . ."

"Give me until the new year," Basil said. He realised he'd shortened his leash, but it was that or nothing. "If I haven't solved it by then, I'll hand it over."

"Fine. West wasn't too keen on working this week anyway." Morris pushed himself out of his chair. "But come January the first, you're handing over the files."

"Yes, sir."

Basil tightened his lips as he watched Morris lumber out of the office. A moment later, he sprang to his feet in search of the man at the front desk. "Has a Mr. Latham checked in?" he asked. "He's the bomb expert I called for the bookshop explosion."

The officer flipped through a pile of notes, then pinched one, lifting it into the air. "Yes, sir. He's in the evidence room as we speak."

The evidence room had long walls lined with shelves stacked with boxes labelled with names and dates referring to specific crimes. A table in the middle of the room was lit with two hanging electric light bulbs, and Basil found Mr. Latham seated there.

"Mr. Latham?" Basil said.

The man's round head bobbed towards Basil's voice. "Chief Inspector! You see, despite the blasted snow, I've kept my word to return after Boxin' Day."

"And for that, I'm grateful." Basil eyed the

shrapnel Latham had displayed on the table. "Have you managed to piece something together?"

"These bits of metal once comprised the cylinder that contained the jump capsule tube and detonator."

"To clarify," Basil said, "it was actually a hand bomb used in the war?"

"Oh, yes indeed." The man's eyes flashed with excitement. He pointed to the long splinter Basil had collected. "This is part of a 'ollow stem—quite extraordinary that a piece remained intact—through which a cord was threaded."

From a small dish, he fished out a trace of thread with a pair of tweezers. "This is all that's left of that. But this—" He returned the thread to the dish and used the tweezers to point to a small stone the size of a kidney bean, and a small, charred spring beside it. "One would release the spring, which loosened the stone, which had the cord tied to it. Then one would pull the cord, triggerin' the detonator, giving one approximately five seconds to throw the bomb. I'd say at least thirty feet away if one didn't want to get injured too."

"I don't recall seeing such an apparatus attached to a hand bomb while in the field," Basil said. "Mind you, I was only in France for one battle." Basil didn't bother to explain that he'd been invalided and now had a tender abdomen and a missing spleen. He was grateful when Latham didn't pry.

"No, yer wouldn't have, I suspect," Latham said as he rubbed the back of his neck. "This is a *Brennzünder* 24."

"Brennzünder?" Basil gaped at the man. "Are you saying the bomb is German?"

"I am, sir. And I'm quite shocked to find evidence of one 'ere in London, especially after all these years. And this is interesting." Latham produced a magnifying glass. "Take a closer look at the grooves in the cylinder shrapnel."

Basil did as instructed, squinting at the image enlarged behind the glass. He stared up at Latham. "Sand?"

15

Though Ginger adored the Christmas season, she was also happy when all the celebrations were over, especially this time, with the added difficulties brought on by the snow. One needed a moment to breathe before the next big to-do, only a few days away. She loved hosting parties at Hartigan House and enjoyed planning the New Year's Eve bash with Felicia, but a hot thread of worry curled in her stomach as she contemplated cancelling. Ginger loved the snow, but why couldn't it have come before Christmas or after New Year's Day? Such dratted bad timing.

However, the weather was the one thing man couldn't control, no matter how modern the world now was or how advanced science had become.

Ginger was content to relax in the arms of her hand-some husband in the sitting room in front of a toasty fire, with Boss curled up beside her.

The sitting room was her favourite place to unwind. The furniture curled towards a large stone fireplace, always lit over the winter months. A Waterhouse painting hung over the hearth, *The Mermaid*, which featured a mystical red-headed creature that reminded Ginger of a painting done of her late mother. Tall, south-facing windows let in an abundance of natural light, and a sideboard on the opposite wall was always stocked with brandy and other spirits and clean crystal glasses.

Ginger and Haley had spent a lot of time working on cases when they'd first arrived from Boston. When Haley returned to America, Basil had gradually taken her spot. Haley seemed to have a sense that this time was meant for Ginger and Basil, and despite Ginger's protests, had graciously excused herself after a quick drink and retired to her room where she swore she had a pile of reading to do.

After a sip of brandy, the drink Ginger and Basil both enjoyed at the end of a long day, she said, "I love spending time with the children, but spending Boxing Day without our servants, especially without

Nanny Green, made me appreciate our staff all the more."

Basil chuckled. "I've grown rather attached to the lot of them myself."

Ginger held back a laugh. When she and Basil had begun their courtship, he lived alone in his Mayfair townhouse with no servants. Marrying her and moving into Hartigan House had been a significant change for him and evidence of his love for her.

"At least Mrs. Beasley had left a lot of food in the refrigerator."

Basil patted his belly. "And delicious food indeed."

Ginger gazed at her husband, now curious about his day. "How was work? Any news about the case?"

Basil inhaled deeply, then said, "Morris doesn't want me on the case."

Ginger stared in alarm. "Don't tell me. Conflict of interest?"

"Indeed. I argued that I wasn't related to Miss Hartigan, had never even met her, and because Pippins was on the staff where I lived, he would likely be more open to speaking to me when he awoke than a stranger."

"And Morris relented on those grounds?"

"He gave me until the new year," Basil grunted.

"I believe he doesn't want to be bothered assigning my replacement during the run-up to New Year."

"That's only a week," Ginger murmured.

"I know." Basil sipped his drink. "The bomb expert came to the Yard today."

"Mr. Latham? Despite the snow?"

"The same. It turns out the hand bomb originated in Germany."

Ginger cringed. "Are you certain?"

"Quite. The Germans attach a stick to theirs to aid in throwing velocity and accuracy. I have to admire the ingenuity."

"I'm surprised the place didn't catch fire."

"There's a reason for that," Basil said. "German grenades were intended to produce a concussive force rather than heat. They're not a typical fragmentation bomb."

"I'm just happy Pippins survived," Ginger said. She regretted not making it to the hospital to visit him that day, but Haley had assured her that rest and quiet were what he needed right now.

"Latham had an explanation for that, too," Basil said. "Pippins must've been bent down, closer to the floor. The thrust of the blast went over him."

"But straight into cousin Florence," Ginger said. "What on earth was she mixed up in?"

Basil shook his head. "I wish we knew."

Talk of the case had caused Ginger to liven up, the fatigue she'd felt only minutes earlier ebbing away. She shifted in her seat, moving Boss to the side so she could face Basil head-on. "Let's review what we know, shall we? Do you still have the piece of paper with the riddle on it?"

"It's in evidence."

"That's all right," Ginger said. "I remember it. *My spine is stiff, my poetry stale.* Spine can mean one's back or the spine of a book, and with the allusion to poetry, cousin Florence would've assumed the latter. *I'm as old as these streets; I tell many a tale . . .*"

"Hatchards is the oldest bookshop in London," Basil said. "She followed the clue to the right place."

Ginger continued reciting. *"There's one about oceans without any tide. At Times, vast foreign countries, where no one abides."*

"References to travel," Basil said. "It took her to the correct section."

"Atlas," Ginger said. "Atlases are large and heavy. Perhaps, as she pulled the largest one off the shelf, it was rigged to cause other books to fall."

"That would account for the five seconds needed before the bomb went off," Basil said. "I wondered why they hadn't noticed the bomb when the book was pulled off the shelf. It had to have pulled the cord which ignited it."

"The books falling to the ground would've distracted cousin Florence, who was balancing on the ladder. Pippins, being a gentleman, would've immediately attempted to recover the books."

Basil shifted in his seat. "A move which quite likely saved his life."

"Dear Pippins," Ginger said with a pout. "He received a message from cousin Florence that day, which took him to the book shop. He and cousin Florence would've had to walk past Miss Gibbons, who was working on the sales counter."

"Mr. Jennings, being short of staff, might've missed seeing them head to the travel section," Basil said. "Though he does seem like the type of fellow who doesn't miss much."

"But how and when was the bomb set up?" Ginger asked. "I suppose anyone could've broken in and done it."

"Jennings did report an untrustworthy employee," Basil said. "Braxton and I called in to see the fellow, a Mr. Will Crockett."

"And what were your impressions?" Ginger asked.

"The man's got a tight relationship with the drink, I'm afraid."

"That kind of situation could lead a man to do something he wouldn't have otherwise."

"Indeed, though he did have a troubling war injury," Basil said. "Damage to his right hand. I'm not sure if it's severe enough to prevent him from setting up the bomb, though it is hard to imagine him being able to."

"It feels like we're going around in circles." Ginger pushed locks of hair behind both ears. "Perhaps a trip to Great Yarmouth is in order?"

Basil jerked backwards. "Are you serious? In this weather?"

"The trains are still running, are they not? Besides, something brought cousin Florence to London, and I'm starting to believe it wasn't me. I'm embarrassed to say my invitation to her came from a letter she sent me to reacquaint herself with us."

"Do you think she was looking for a legitimate reason to meet up with Pippins?"

"Perhaps." Ginger hummed. "Pippins has been talking in his delirium. He appears to be locked somewhere in the past, during the years he worked for cousin Florence. I can't help but wonder if someone there knows something. What happened during those years? And could the past be related to current events somehow?"

"It's not a bad idea, love," Basil said. "Let's sleep on it, shall we?" He rose to his feet, extending his hand. She took it, letting him guide her up the staircase. Boss followed behind, his nails making soft clacking sounds on the tiled floor as he went.

When Ginger awakened the next morning, she found that Basil was already up and gone from the bedroom. Ginger dressed quickly in a woollen tunic with long sleeves and a high collar to defend herself against the cold and, inspired by Haley's modern thinking, a new pair of lady's trousers. Feeling an urgent curiosity, she wondered if Basil had learned something new about the case. In her haste, she nearly bumped into him as she stepped into the corridor.

"Basil? Is everything all right?"

"Splendid, love. I rang the Yard to inform them that the case was leading me to Great Yarmouth and that I would be away for a few days."

Ginger felt a warm flare of excitement. Deep down, she sensed they'd learn something important there. Cousin Florence and possibly Pippins were the keys to unlocking this secret. "I'll need some time to pack," she said as she pivoted back into the bedroom. She rang the bell for Lizzie. "I shall have her pack for you as well."

"Jolly good," Basil said. "I'll meet you in the morning room when you're ready to eat breakfast."

Nanny Green reassured Ginger that Rosa would be fine without her mummy for a few days, and Scout, who'd always been self-sufficient, announced he'd be busy caring for the two horses on the property.

Clement and Marvin shovelled a path from the front door to the street, but that didn't help with the snow blocking a taxicab from making it down the cul-de-sac.

"The driver will have to park on the road," Basil said. "We'll make our way to him."

This decision led to Basil instructing their shovelling crew to continue their efforts along the pavement. Thankfully, it wasn't a long way.

"At least the snowfall has stopped," Ginger said, "but the wind is dreadfully chilly."

After confirming with Haley and Felicia that they'd take turns checking up on Pippins and to "be sure to telegraph if he worsens", Ginger and Basil made a brisk walk to the taxicab when it arrived and climbed into the back seat.

"Liverpool Street station," Basil instructed.

Ginger placed a gloved hand on his arm. "Perhaps we should pop in and see Pippins before we go? He might've come round overnight. He may offer pertinent information."

Basil checked his wristwatch. "An extra hour won't hurt, I suppose, but I had hoped to get there before dark."

"I feel it might be important," Ginger insisted. "We can book a room in Norwich if necessary and travel to Great Yarmouth in the morning."

Basil conceded and gave the driver new instructions to proceed to the hospital. Ginger breathed out her relief. She'd feel so much better leaving if she could get assurances for herself that Pippins was on the mend.

As providence would have it, they caught the doctor as he was leaving Pippins' room.

"Good day, Mrs. Reed, Chief Inspector," he said when he spotted them.

"Good day," Ginger returned, her gaze darting to Pippins' hospital room door. "How is our dear Pippins today?"

"His arm is healing nicely, so that is good news,

though I'm afraid that conk on the head will take more time."

Basil gripped his hat in his hands. "Is he still unconscious?"

"In and out," the doctor replied. "Only because of the medicines he's on, but he's making reasonable progress considering his age and the nature of his injury."

"Is it all right if we see him now?" Ginger asked. When the doctor hesitated, she added, "We won't stay long."

"Very well. As I said, he's medicated, so don't be alarmed if he doesn't make a lot of sense."

Quietly, Ginger stepped into Pippins' room with Basil close behind her. Pippins still had his arm in a cast, but the bandages on his head had been reduced, and his pallor had improved.

"I think he looks a bit better," Ginger said, "though he's getting awfully thin."

"We'll get him home soon," Basil said. "And fatten him up again."

Ginger offered Basil a soft smile of appreciation before taking Pippins' cold hand. "Dear Pippins, it's Mr. and Mrs. Reed."

"What ho, old chap," Basil said through a forced smile.

Ginger shot him a look.

"I'm sorry, love. Hospitals make me nervous."

Ginger turned back to Pippins. "Pips, Mr. Reed and I are taking a trip up to Great Yarmouth. To see Miss Hartigan's place." Ginger didn't want to say that her cousin had died. That sad information could wait until Pippins' mind was clear.

Pippins squeezed her hand, and Ginger smiled. "He can hear us," she said. "He squeezed my hand."

"Miss Hartigan." Pippins' voice was low and raspy. "We should tell Mrs. Underhill. No, no, you're right. It would be careless of us."

Ginger's sense of joy evaporated into concern. "Pippins?"

"The authorities . . . they'll catch us . . ."

Ginger shot Basil a look of alarm before saying again, "Pippins?"

"Dear, dear," Pippins It's "It's not your fault." His breath quickened as he fell deeper into sleep.

16

*W*e've been hiding a German man and his sister on the upper floor of The Willows for over a year. Once I'd informed Miss Hartigan about my suspicions regarding an extra room behind the tapestry, she decided to confide in me. We agreed that forcing the siblings to remain in a single room, day and night, was more torturous than actual internment by the British and allowed them the freedom to roam upstairs once the staff had gone home for the evening. Since none of the staff besides myself live full-time in the house, it was easy to announce that the upper floor would be shut up to conserve energy during the war. Miss Hartigan naturally wouldn't be doing any entertaining, especially with overnight guests, so her edict wasn't considered unusual at first.

Tobias and Hilde Schubert are making the most of their time hiding at The Willows. Miss Hartigan provides reading material, board games, and even a gramophone which can only be played once the house is empty.

As time passes, the situation is growing more precarious in two ways. First, the police have become more militant as the war drags on, and the sentiment towards anyone with the misfortune of originating from certain European countries has grown increasingly antagonistic, especially towards the Germans, and especially since the Zeppelin bombings over England.

I recall the first time the bombings happened last year. The Zeppelins had been driven off course by strong winds and ended up dropping their bombs on the villages and towns of Norfolk, including Great Yarmouth. My heart races as I remember how we all took cover in the cellar at The Willows, praying that we'd escape harm. A day later, the news had reported that two British aircraft had tried but failed to find the airships. A total of four people were killed in the attacks.

Being born in Great Britain, as Tobias Schubert was, isn't enough to save a person with German ancestry, either. Anyone with parents, grandparents, and even great-grandparents with German or Austro-Hungarian heritage is now persona non grata. They are rounded up and imprisoned. Miss Hilde, the eldest sibling, has the misfortune of being born in her homeland, though she has lived in England since infancy. Her fate, if caught, wouldn't be internment camps but exile back to the Continent where the ravages of war are more severe, and the difficulties for a single woman would be immense.

The second danger lies within Miss Hartigan's heart, as she and Mr. Tobias Schubert have strong romantic feelings for each other. A shared crisis can push a couple together more quickly and intensely than in normal times.

Mrs. Underhill has known all along. Miss Hartigan has the housekeeper's loyalty. Hiding what amounts to fugitives from the government isn't something one can succeed at on one's own. Once I discovered the truth and professed my allegiance to Miss Hartigan, Mrs. Underhill's antagonism towards me subsided greatly.

Because of Penny and Finch, we are keeping up appearances, preparing for Christmas of 1916 as if it was just another wartime Christmas.

"The mistress is feeling extra hungry again today," I say. "I'll take the plate to her sitting room when you have it ready." It isn't my job to serve the meals, nor the cook's job to deliver them. But we can't ask Penny to do it.

"Such a shame she never comes to the dining room to eat," Mrs. Underhill says. "But I suppose it's no fun eating alone." She catches my eye as she hands me Miss Hartigan's tray. "And you'll help yourself later?"

"The same as always," I say. "Miss Hartigan wishes to extend her thanks," I add. "For doing so much with so little."

This produces the hint of a smile. "We all have to do our bit, eh?"

"We do," I agree. "I'll see you tomorrow."

Mrs. Underhill will clean up what little mess was made in the kitchen, then head home to her family. I nod, passing Penny in the corridor, and say, "Mrs. Underhill requires your help in the kitchen."

"I know, Mr. Pippins," she says wearily. "I'm on my way."

I like to wait until the maid has gone before making a plate of dinner for myself. Everything has been unconventional since the war started, but it means I can serve up extra for Mr. Schubert without encountering Penny or Finch, should he enter the kitchen. But first, I have to deliver Miss Hartigan's supper, which she shares with Mr. Schubert's sister.

Miss Hartigan sits in the sitting room connected to her bedroom, where she waits thrice a day. Her dull eyes slightly brighten when she sees me. For someone who supposedly overeats at each meal, Miss Hartigan is becoming frightfully thin, and even her frock, with its long narrow sleeves, small waist, and long flowing skirt, can no longer conceal the fact. I'm not the only one to notice it, surely.

Miss Hartigan stretches her neck to look past me into the corridor. "You're certain the coast is clear?"

I step into the doorway and cast another look. "Yes, miss. Mrs. Underhill and Penny are in the kitchen. Finch is outside."

Miss Hartigan follows me as I carry the tray, side-stepping the areas that squeak as we walk to the heavy-hanging tapestry at the end of the corridor. Handing the tray to Miss Hartigan, I lift one side away from the wall and do our secret knock. Mr. Schubert cracks the door open just wide enough for Miss Hartigan to slip inside. I can't miss the look of affection that passes between them. Miss Schubert watches them from behind, her dark eyes flashing with contempt.

I ponder the lack of gratitude the sister displays as the door closes silently and the tapestry falls back into place. She clearly doesn't like her brother growing close to the person saving both their lives. Miss Hilde Schubert seems quite attached to her brother, and perhaps the stress of the situation is making her reluctant to enjoy the happiness of others. I can only imagine how difficult it must be to be locked up like a prisoner when you've done nothing but been born in the wrong country.

By the time I arrive with my dinner and a plate for Mr. Schubert—Miss Hartigan insists that I eat with them as we are breaking protocol anyway—they are sitting in the upper sitting room, with only a few candles lit and the gramophone playing a scratchy record at low volume.

Mr. Schubert is always polite, agreeable, and profusely expresses his thanks.

Miss Schubert seems to have little control over her emotions and often gives in to emotional outbursts.

"I'm so bloody bored," she proclaims with a dramatic sigh. "It's not the blasted war that will kill me but enduring the wait for it to end." She stares at her brother. "Tobias?"

"You can't expect me to know when it will end,"

Mr. Schubert says heavily. "And when it eventually does end, as all wars are bound to, I can hardly say what will happen to us then. The hearts and minds of the British people won't warm up to us overnight."

"But they will," Miss Hartigan insists. She reaches for Mr. Schubert's hand, then pulls it away, blushing at the fact she almost demonstrated her affection for the German in the presence of Miss Schubert and me.

Dramatically Miss Schubert says, "I might kill myself by then."

Mr. Schubert protests. "Hilde!"

"I am joking, Tobias," she returns snidely.

"Only men are being interred, Miss Schubert," I say rather daringly. "You could go on with your life elsewhere, if you wish, with the proper disguise."

"I would rather die than be separated from my brother, Pippins." Her emphasis on my name makes it clear that she, though the fugitive, is above me, a mere butler, in social class. I finish my meal in silence after that.

The next day is a Sunday, which means the staff have the day off. Miss Hartigan encourages me to take the day off too, but I still feel like a newcomer to the town and have no family or friends in the area. I'd

*just as soon stay at The Willows and continue my
duties.*

*Since the staff have gone, and the house is rather
isolated at the south end of Great Yarmouth, one can
count on a good amount of privacy. Sundays are the
only day that the Schuberts venture outside. They
don't go far, just a jaunt down the beach. At first, they
go out alone, but recently Miss Hartigan has been
going with them. I heard her tell Mr. Schubert that
she can't bear the worry that they'd one day be spotted, and if she were with them, she could advocate, or
at the very least, spin a believable story that he and
Hilde are her English relations.*

*I don't like how deeply Miss Hartigan has
become involved in the subterfuge. The more lies she
tells, the more complicit she becomes. The law will
come after her as furiously as it would Tobias Schubert, and that makes me nervous.*

*When the party returns in the afternoon, Miss
Hartigan is in an elevated level of distress. The winter
mist off the North Sea has caused the broad brim of
her hat to sag toward her shoulders, and the hem of her
loose-fitting wool coat, caked in sand, hangs limply at
her ankles.*

"What is it, miss?" I ask.

"It's Miss Schubert. She's disappeared."

"I don't understand." I peer out of the window and glance down the beach, hoping Miss Schubert will magically appear, which, of course, she doesn't. "How could she disappear?"

Miss Hartigan's cheeks grow rosy with unease. "Mr. Schubert and I were talking together, and Miss Schubert lagged. I'm embarrassed to say we were quite—"

My mind fills in her pause with the word "enamoured", but she continues with "engaged".

"We were quite engaged in conversation, and well, we didn't notice when she was no longer part of our company."

"Where is Mr. Schubert now?" I ask.

"He's searching for her and quite beside himself with worry. And now I'm worried about him." Miss Hartigan blinks hard. "As you said last night, it's the men who are in danger. If they catch him, they'll put him in prison." Her hand moves to her throat. "I just can't bear the thought of something happening to him, of not seeing him again."

We both blush at Miss Hartigan's sudden unfiltered emotion. She stares nervously at her hand. "Forgive—"

"How about a cup of tea, miss?" I say, interrupting her unnecessary apology. "Shall I put the kettle on?" *To do so isn't in line with my duties, but the circumstances are hardly normal.*

"Yes, Pippins, yes," she answers with relief. "That would be nice."

I deliver a cup of tea which Miss Hartigan drinks with gratitude. At that moment, Mr. Schubert breezes through the door. "I've found her," he says with agitation. "With a man!"

Miss Hartigan almost drops her tea, and I quickly move to relieve her of the cup. "A man?" she repeats. "What man?"

Miss Schubert steps in behind Mr. Schubert and casually removes her coat and scarf. I resist the urge to do my usual duty and take them from her, knowing she needs to take all her belongings upstairs.

"Tobias is making a mountain out of a molehill," she says.

"I am making a mountain?" he returns with eyes round with disbelief. "You were speaking to a strange English man. We are hiding from everyone English!"

"It was nothing. Just a diversion. I can sound very British when I want to. Honestly, it was just a little harmless flirting. Besides, I needed a break from watching you two lovebirds cooing at each other."

Miss Hartigan gasps. Mr. Schubert takes Miss

Schubert's arm and none too gently leads her back upstairs.

I'm worried that Miss Schubert's recklessness will be our undoing.

The following day, Miss Hartigan asks me to drive her into town to do some shopping. With Christmas of 1916 approaching, there is more to consider than on a usual Saturday. Finch, who usually drives her, has the afternoon off. Miss Hartigan is one of the rare civilians who owns a motorcar, a 1913 Benz 8/20 HP Roadster with seating for two, but doesn't like to drive it herself. I turn the crank as she waits in the back.

Though the motorcar is quicker than the traditional horse and carriage, it still takes a good twenty minutes to return to civilisation. Miss Hartigan stops at a dress shop, where she purchases gifts whilst I wait.

I'm storing her packages in the boot of the motorcar when a pair of bobbies stroll up, batons in hand. One of them says, "Miss Hartigan, the chief constable would like a word."

My heart nearly drops to my shoes. Miss Hartigan's hand goes to her throat. "Why on earth would the chief constable want to speak to me?"

"I'm afraid I don't know, madam. Only that

should we spot you shopping at some point this week, we were supposed to bring you in."

I secure the lid of the boot, then say, "I'll drive you there, miss."

Miss Hartigan, looking paler than she usually does this time of year, simply nods. I open the passenger door for her, and she gets in.

The interview is worse than I could have imagined. The chief constable gets right to the point and accuses Miss Hartigan of harbouring war criminals.

"I'm doing no such thing!" In Miss Hartigan's mind, the Schuberts aren't war criminals. They are war victims. "How can you even suggest such a thing?"

"We have our ways, miss," the chief constable says, "eyes and ears, here and there."

"Well, am I under arrest?"

For clarity, I add, "Are we?"

"Not yet," the chief constable says, "but I wanted to let you know that I'm sending men to your house to have a look around. If you're as innocent as you say, you won't mind a small inconvenience."

Miss Hartigan lifts her chin at her supposed affront. I offer a hand to assist her from her chair, and she walks out of the police station with all the dignity she can muster. When we reach the motorcar and are seated inside, she looks at me and says, "Drive as fast as you can, Pippins. We must warn Mr. and Miss Schubert that trouble is on its way."

I do my best to honour Miss Hartigan's request. I try too hard, and when a stray goat darts across the road, I swerve sharply to miss it, sending the motorcar into the ditch. A large bush conceals the crash site. Thankfully, neither of us is seriously hurt, just a little shaken. Our nerves are shot further as we spot a police motorcar rumble on by.

17

*L*eaving Pippins was difficult, but Ginger just knew that somehow the answers she and Basil sought would be found on the east coast.

"It was so unsettling how disturbed he became at the end of our visit," Ginger said once she and Basil were settled in the back of the taxicab. "I hope we didn't do more harm than good."

"He did let us know a few things," Basil said. "That he and Miss Hartigan were afraid of the police and didn't want to tell a Mrs. Underhill about it."

Ginger stared blankly out of the window. "I can hardly imagine what Pippins and Florence could've done that would warrant apprehension by the police."

Basil rubbed the back of his neck. "Who would've ever imagined that Pippins and Miss Hartigan would somehow be involved in a shop bombing? Those two were entangled in something."

"And whatever that was," Ginger said, "I'm determined to find it out."

The taxicab driver turned on to Liverpool Street, sliding a little on the slick road as he yanked the steering wheel to bring the machine back in line. After paying the man, they exited the cab and, with large flakes of snow landing on their shoulders, headed for the Great Eastern Railway line. Ginger and Basil bought two first-class tickets to Norwich, where they would catch a connecting train to Great Yarmouth.

"It'll be dark by the time we arrive," Basil said. "I suggest we stay the night at a hotel and head to Miss Hartigan's residence in the morning."

Though Ginger was eager to get to cousin Florence's house by the sea—she imagined it would be lovely—snowy roads could be problematic, so delaying their departure until they could travel in the light of day made sense.

With its long platforms and high ceilings, the station felt cavernous, and noise echoed around it. Numerous passengers, looking tired and frustrated, were being given news of more delays. A porter transported their luggage to the luggage carriage. Ginger and Basil boarded first class, found their compartment and sat on clean, upholstered seats hat provided sufficient comfort.

Ginger perused the itinerary. "We'll head through Chelmsford, Colchester, and Ipswich," she said. "I suppose Pippins would've taken this same route all those years ago."

"That's quite likely," Basil agreed.

"Though not in first class." Ginger imagined a slightly younger Pippins, seated on a wooden bench in third class, regularly shifting to ease his physical discomfort and staring out the window. Was he nervous about starting his new life in Norfolk—set to work for a spinster he'd never met? "It was rather brave of him," Ginger mused. "My father pulled the strings from Boston, removing him from London to the unknown."

"I'd wager Pippins was thankful to stay employed," Basil said. "Especially in those years. Many households significantly reduced their staff."

After a while, Ginger and Basil headed to the dining car and enjoyed a leisurely meal of steak and kidney pie. The entire trip, including the connecting train ride, was dreadfully long, the weather making a five-hour trip take eight hours. By the time they reached Great Yarmouth, Ginger was quite ready to get off the rattling train and onto solid ground. She was pleased when the porter told them about a reputable inn nearby.

The Nelson Inn was large enough to be considered a hotel but maintained the quaintness of a country establishment. The manor-like exterior was heavily decorated for Christmas with plenty of lights and green boughs of holly and mistletoe. The interior was similar but with the addition of Father Christmas ornaments set in corners and paper chains attached in loops along the shelves.

The innkeeper was a dapper fellow in his sixties, around the same age Pippins would've been when he lived there. He wore a suit with tails, shiny black shoes, and white gloves. His greying hair was parted dramatically on one side and combed with oil to the other. A set of gold-framed spectacles were perched on an up-tipped nose. He greeted Ginger and Basil with a hearty "Merry Christmas and Happy New Year!" and "This weather is dreadful, but at least it means I have plenty of rooms for you to choose from."

Ginger thought that fortuitous indeed. "Thank you, Mr.—"

"Watts."

"Would it still be possible to have some dinner?" Basil asked.

"Certainly, sir," Mr. Watts said. "The seafood is always on special."

"That sounds good to me," Ginger said. Her stomach protested as it had been quite a while since the lunch they had had on the train.

"Just let me register you folks in, and George will take your luggage to your room." Ginger glanced at a tall boy dressed in a uniform and hat. He dropped his gaze to the ground shyly.

"Could I have your names, please?"

Basil answered, "Mr. and Mrs. Reed."

Mr. Watts glanced up over his spectacles. "And how long will you be staying?"

When Basil looked at Ginger, she responded with a slight lift of her right shoulder. "We need to be back by New Year's Eve."

"Ah, right," Basil returned. "The party." To Mr. Watts, he added, "Can we play it by ear? Perhaps one to three nights?"

For the first time, the innkeeper lost his look of cheer. "So, you're not here to celebrate New Year with friends and family?"

"Oh yes," Ginger said, hoping to reassure the

man. "We're visiting my cousin's place in the morning."

If the man thought Ginger's wording was odd, he made no sign of it. "Very good," he said. He announced their room number and gave them a key. "I do hope you enjoy your stay."

"Thank you," Ginger said. "Mr. Watts, would you mind if we asked you a few questions?"

"About Great Yarmouth? I'd be happy to. I've lived here my whole life, know the streets like the back of my hand, and all the places visitors like to go."

"I'm hoping to learn about my family history," Ginger offered. "Especially during the Great War. Did you run this inn then?"

"Oh yes, madam. Those were terrible times, indeed. Not when it started, but after the first year, it was frightfully difficult to get supplies. The North Sea was particularly dangerous as it's a clear and easy route for the enemy to reach us."

"Does the name Florence Hartigan mean anything to you?" Ginger asked.

The innkeeper twisted his lips as he strained to remember. "I don't think so, madam. No, wait. Hartigan. There was something. Had to do with the Germans."

Ginger gave Basil a sideways glance before asking, "What Germans?"

"I don't know. Friends of hers, perhaps. In those days, it was against the law to house Germans and Austro-Hungarians. They were rounded up in internment camps." Mr. Watts snapped his fingers. "There was one newspaper story about a German woman who took a rowing boat and met a German vessel. A witness said she was brought on board, only to be pushed into the sea." He nodded glumly. "Drowned."

The bell over the door rang as another guest entered the inn, cutting their conversation short. "Thank you, Mr. Watts," Ginger said.

"Any time, madam. If you have any other questions, I'd be happy to help."

As Ginger and Basil headed to their room, Ginger's mind spun. Had cousin Florence and Pippins defied the law during the war by hiding war fugitives? And if so, what did that have to do with the bombing at Hatchards bookshop?

irst thing after breakfast, Ginger and Basil hired a motorcar and headed to cousin Florence's residence, a few miles to the south. Warmer temperatures had turned the snow to rain and snowbanks to slush, causing a treacherous ride. On one particularly close call with a ditch, Ginger grabbed her hat and shot Basil a nervous look. "Don't take this the wrong way, love," she said, "but perhaps I should drive."

Basil choked back a laugh. "Please don't take this the wrong way, love, but there's no way on God's green earth that I'm going to let you drive."

Ginger hardly knew what to make of Basil's shocking response but pushed it out of her mind as the task at hand had to take precedence. She spoke loudly over the noise of the engine. "In her letters, cousin Florence referred to her residence as The Willows. Apparently, there is a grove of willows in the back garden."

The road ran parallel to the sea, which was white with caps that met a brooding winter sky. A ray of sunlight would break blue and purple clouds, reflecting off the sea's surface like a specular gem. The breathtaking beauty made Ginger miss living by the ocean as she had in Boston.

Finally, a house came into view: only two storeys and a gabled attic. "Is that it?" Ginger asked. At first, she thought they mustn't have the correct address, but when spotted the weathered sign with the words "The Willows" written in faded script, she realised they had arrived. Indeed, there were willow trees in sight. "Cousin Florence came from Hartigan money," Ginger said. "I'd imagined something bigger."

"Perhaps it was big enough for a spinster," Basil said as he turned down the short drive. "Lovely location, I'll say."

Ginger couldn't disagree with that. Miles of uninhabited beach stretched in both directions. Other residences were in sight, each on its own large parcel of land.

Bracing herself in the wind, Ginger tightened her fur coat and folded her arms to hold in the warmth. Even with the embellishment of a snow-trimmed rooftop, the house looked tired, in need of fresh paint, and beneath the thin blanket of snow, the garden had remnants of dried autumn foliage broken by the wind and scattered about.

"Perhaps the gardener is on a Christmas break," Basil said.

"If cousin Florence still retains a gardener," Ginger returned. "I assumed she still retained a full staff, but I really don't know. Have the police informed the household of cousin Florence's demise?"

"I would hope an attempt was made," Basil said, "but as it was Christmas, they might've been hard to track down."

Ginger wondered if there was anyone on the premises. The moody winter morning made daytime lighting desirable, and the house appeared dark. If someone was in, perhaps they were at the back of the house or in the cellar.

Basil led the way to the front door and used the wrought-iron knocker to announce their presence. After his third attempt, Ginger was worried that they'd made the trip for nothing when suddenly the door cracked open.

A woman wearing a simple day frock with a fine-knit jumper over sloped shoulders stared back with worried eyes.

"Yes?" she said tentatively.

Ginger answered, "I'm Mrs. Reed. Miss Hartigan's cousin. This is my husband, Mr. Reed."

The woman blinked back in confusion. "I don't understand. I thought Miss Hartigan was staying with you over Christmas."

"Might we come in?" Ginger said kindly.

"Of course, where are my manners?" the woman replied. "I'm just surprised." Once the door was closed and they stood inside the entranceway, the woman said, "I'm Mrs. Underhill, the cook and housekeeper. Let me show you to the drawing room. I'll make you some tea."

"Would you bring three cups?" Ginger said. "Please join us."

Mrs. Underhill's eyes darkened as if she knew bad news was coming, but she nodded without protesting.

The drawing room was comfortably furnished with the requisite fireplace and a wireless cabinet in the corner. "One would have to enjoy solitude to live alone in this house and so far from town," Basil said.

"Cousin Florence probably counted her staff as friends. I'm not looking forward to telling Mrs. Underhill about my cousin's fate," Ginger replied.

Soon Mrs. Underhill returned with a tea tray and set it on the low table. "You'll allow me to pour, madam?"

Ginger nodded. Once three cups were poured and sugar added, they took their seats. Mrs. Underhill sat on the edge of a chair with ornately crafted wooden arms and upholstery on the seat and back. She looked uncomfortable. As if she were ready to bolt. She sipped her tea then set it on the table beside her. "I have the feeling you've come with bad news."

"I'm very sorry to say that's true," Ginger said, placing her teacup to the side. "There was an accident in London, and Miss Hartigan did not survive."

Mrs. Underhill pinched her eyes shut as her lower lip quivered. Ginger went to her side, offering a handkerchief. "I'm so very sorry," she said.

Mrs. Underhill accepted the handkerchief and held it to her face, her shoulders shaking as she sobbed silently. Then, with a deep breath, she composed herself. "Forgive me. I'm not normally so emotional. I just . . . it's just so shocking, and now . . ."

Florence's death meant a loss of employment for those who still served her. "I'm sure something will work out," Ginger said. "Who else does Miss Hartigan employ?"

"Just me, Penny the housemaid, and the butler, Mr. Digby. He's visiting family in town. Penny isn't here right now. She's gone to London for Christmas."

Ginger and Basil shared a look. If the maid Penny was in London at the same time as Florence, that could be their first lead.

"When do you expect Penny to return?" Ginger asked.

"Today, if she can get here with this dreadful weather," Mrs. Underhill said. "Oh dear. I'm not looking forward to telling her the sad news."

Ginger stared back with a look of compassion. "Were Penny and Miss Hartigan close?"

"As close as a lady and her maid could be, I suppose. The three of us—Penny, Mr. Finch, and me —have been with Miss Hartigan for many, many years."

"Mr. Finch?"

"Oh yes, he was the gardener. He passed away in

October. Miss Hartigan didn't have the heart to replace him and said it could wait until spring."

Ginger knew that time could cause a family-type of affection to grow between staff and a master or mistress of the house, but the opposite could also be true. Resentment or disdain for one's employer could also fester. But to the point of murder? Ginger believed that was definitely a possibility.

"And Mr. Digby?" she asked.

"He came after the war," Mrs. Underhill said, "but has been serving Miss Hartigan for almost nine years now."

"I'm correct in saying you worked for Miss Hartigan during the Great War?" Basil asked.

"Yes, of course," Mrs. Underhill returned. "A challenging time it was."

"My butler, Mr. Pippins, was in Miss Hartigan's employ at that time," Ginger said.

Mrs. Underhill stilled. "Yes, yes, he was. Mr. Pippins was very . . . er . . . loyal to Miss Hartigan."

"You hesitated on your word choice," Basil said. "Did something happen whilst Mr. Pippins worked here?"

Mrs. Underhill swallowed. "It's not something we speak of."

"Mrs. Underhill," Ginger started. "I'm afraid I

must inform you that Miss Hartigan's death is suspicious."

"Suspicious?" Mrs. Underhill blinked hard. "Are you saying she was *murdered*?"

"It's the premise we're following," Basil said. "So do consider our questions carefully. Please keep in mind that I am a chief inspector at Scotland Yard. Please tell us what you no longer speak of?"

"It's just been so long." Mrs. Underhill's shaky hand went to her throat. "It's almost like it didn't happen."

"What didn't happen, Mrs. Underhill?" Ginger prodded. "It's all right. You can tell us."

"Those German siblings."

Ginger recalled the innkeeper mentioning a German woman had drowned. "Did Miss Hartigan assist them during the war?" Ginger asked.

Mrs. Underhill locked eyes with Ginger. "It was illegal at the time."

"And yet, some chose to break the law," Basil said.

Ginger couldn't think that Florence could've accomplished such a feat without help from her housekeeper. There was no sense implicating the woman in the crime now.

Ginger leaned closer. "What happened to the siblings?"

"Oh, it was in all the news," Mrs. Underhill said. "At least locally. The police got word of it somehow. You can hear and see a motorcar coming from quite a distance, especially from the upper-floor windows. The Schubert siblings tried to escape through the window. There was an old wooden trellis at the time, where clematis grew. Miss Schubert made it down, but it splintered under the weight of Mr. Schubert. He fell on his head, knocking himself out cold. His sister left him behind. He was apprehended by the police and taken to hospital."

Mrs. Underhill's gaze moved towards the ceiling. "You know, I hadn't thought of the Schuberts in years, and then a few weeks ago, I thought I saw Miss Hilda Schubert on the beach. She was digging about in the sand as if searching for cockles. In December, can you imagine? When I went to investigate, she'd already left." After a shrug, she added, "Must've been her doppelgänger."

Ginger shared a look with Basil, then asked, "What happened to Miss Hartigan and Mr. Pippins?"

"They were arrested. But Miss Hartigan had a good solicitor, and somehow, he got them off on a lesser charge. Your Mr. Pippins spent time in jail, but Miss Hartigan got away with a fine."

Ginger shivered at the thought of her poor Pips spending time in jail. All these years, and she'd never known!

"Did you or Mr. Finch or even Penny ever encounter ammunition during those times?" Basil asked.

Mrs. Underhill shot him a perplexed look. "Certainly not! I can't imagine how one would even do that." She picked up her teacup and winced after a sip. "The tea's gone cold. I'll make a fresh pot and bring out some sandwiches for you. It's nearly lunchtime. You must be hungry."

Although her mind whirled, Ginger thanked the housekeeper for her hospitality. Florence and Pippins had hidden enemy aliens. How very courageous of them both.

19

*M*rs. Underhill left Ginger and Basil alone in the dining room to eat lunch. After commenting on the appealing aroma and taste, Ginger said, "What do you make of Mrs. Underhill's story about the German siblings?"

"The war years were difficult for anyone with a German or Austro-Hungarian heritage," Basil returned. "Britain was at war with those countries, so anyone with ties to those nations, even if they were born in Britain, was under suspicion as a potential spy."

Ginger had known this, of course, but simply said, "They were rounded up into internment camps."

"Indeed. As prisoners of war."

"I have heard that some tried to go back to Germany or Hungary to fight for the other side," Ginger added.

Basil pursed his lips as he nodded. "Yes. Very concerning to the government and the Crown."

"I'm curious to know what happened to these siblings, Mr. Schubert and Miss Schubert," Ginger said. "Could it be that Miss Schubert was the woman who died in the North Sea trying to escape?"

"The one the innkeeper mentioned?" Basil said. "Perhaps. There may have been another household in the area harbouring fugitives as well."

"Just how common was the act?" Ginger asked.

"No one really knows."

Ginger emptied the little jug of milk into her teacup. "I think I'll go and ask for a bit more milk."

Basil arched a brow. "Wouldn't Mrs. Underhill expect you to ring the bell for that?"

Ginger was already on her feet with the jug in hand. "I don't want to bother her with such a trivial request. She won't protest even if she wants to. Besides, she may speak more openly without you, a copper, in the room."

The kitchen was in the basement, and Ginger

hesitated before heading down. She stilled at the sound of another voice, conversing with Mrs. Underhill.

"Merry Christmas, Mrs. Underhill," came a female voice. "I got it for you in London."

Creeping, Ginger took another step, just far enough to see the caller, a woman who looked to be in her mid-thirties, with short curly hair, round eyes, and a tight smile. Ginger wondered if this was the maid, Penny, and soon had her thoughts confirmed when Mrs. Underhill said, "Thank you, Penny, but you didn't need to do this."

"I know, but I wanted to."

Ginger didn't want to interrupt this personal exchange, so she waited as Mrs. Underhill opened the present in the shape of a book.

"*Metropolis*," Mrs. Underhill said. "I've heard about this book."

Ginger had as well and found it interesting, perhaps even ironic, that Penny would give a book penned by a German author as a Christmas gift, especially in light of Pippins' past in this house and her and Basil's current case.

"I'll enjoy reading this before bed each night," Mrs. Underhill added. "I have a little something for you." Mrs. Underhill opened a cupboard and removed a small wrapped gift.

Penny cooed when she opened it. "Earrings! Mrs. Underhill!"

"For the New Year's Eve party you're so eager to attend," Mrs. Underhill said.

"They're perfect."

Ginger was touched by the apparent affection shared by the cook and the maid and hated to interrupt, but she and Basil were on a fact-finding mission, and time was of the essence.

"Mrs. Underhill," Ginger said, stepping into view. "So sorry to interrupt. I'm wondering if I could have a bit more milk."

A look of dismay crossed the cook's face, but she quickly controlled it. She took the jug from Ginger. "Of course."

Ginger smiled at the maid, who stared back with a look of surprise. "I'm Mrs. Reed, a cousin of Miss Hartigan. You must be Penny."

Penny bobbed; her gaze focused on the floor. "Yes, madam."

Mrs. Underhill put the milk jug on the table and turned to Penny. "Mrs. Reed and her husband are here for a short visit. I'm afraid they have sad news."

"Miss Hartigan has, unfortunately, passed away. There was a mishap in London."

Penny kept her gaze glued to the floor. "That is terrible, madam. I had heard about her demise while in London."

"Penny!" Mrs. Underhill said, looking stunned. "Why didn't you say anything?"

"I didn't want to spoil the gift exchange, Mrs. Underhill. I thought there was time enough for bad news."

Ginger eyed the book on the counter, the gift from Penny to Mrs. Underhill. A bookmark placed inside the cover had the shop name of Hatchards peeking out.

"You were at Hatchards recently, Penny?" she asked.

Penny spoke without looking up. "Yes, madam. I heard about the explosion. Thankfully, it happened after I'd shopped there. I didn't hear that it was Miss Hartigan who was killed until just yesterday."

"I understand you worked for Miss Hartigan during the war years."

Penny shot Mrs. Underhill a look of alarm. Mrs. Underhill nodded as if giving her consent to speak.

"Yes, madam, I did."

"So, you're aware that Miss Hartigan, with the help of Mr. Pippins—her butler at the time—concealed a brother and sister who were wanted by the government."

"Only after the police came, madam."

"You didn't have reason to suspect there were more people upstairs than Miss Hartigan, whilst doing your duties as a maid?"

"Miss Hartigan told me not to go upstairs, that she was closing it off to save money. Everyone had to economise during those days."

"You never met or spoke to Mr. Schubert or Miss Schubert?"

"No, madam. I never met either of them. No one was more surprised than me, madam, to learn people like that had been living in this house all that time, and me being completely unaware. 'Course, Miss Hartigan put me on shorter shifts during the war."

"Do you think there's a connection between the Schuberts and what happened to Miss Hartigan in London, Mrs. Reed?" Mrs. Underhill asked. "It seems rather unlikely, doesn't it?"

Ginger had had the same thought, but said, "We don't want to leave any stone unturned."

"Of course not," Mrs. Underhill said. "Now, why

don't I make you a fresh pot of tea and bring this extra milk with me this time?"

"Actually," Ginger said. "I think it's time for Mr. Reed and me to take our leave. Lunch was delightful, but we would hate to impose on your kindness any longer." She smiled. "Please accept our gratitude."

20

They found Mr. Digby at the address Mrs. Underhill had given them in Great Yarmouth. A middle-aged man wearing a heavy cardigan, and loose trousers held up by wide braces, opened the door. "Yes?" he enquired politely.

After Basil introduced them, Ginger added, "Would you mind if we asked you a few questions?"

"Not at all," Mr. Digby said. "Please come in. Can I offer you a cup of tea?"

"We've actually had our fill of tea at the hands of Mrs. Underhill," Ginger said sweetly. "And lunch. But please make one for yourself if you like."

"I have a cup already made, madam." He motioned for Ginger and Basil to sit across from his chair, which had a teacup on the table beside it.

"Is there news of Miss Hartigan?" he asked tentatively. "I hope she's all right, but your visit, though welcome, is cause for worry."

"I'm afraid our news isn't good," Ginger said. "Miss Hartigan has passed away."

"Oh dear. Oh dear. Oh dear." He pinched his eyes then recovered himself. "That's terrible news indeed."

"We can give you a bit of time," Basil said, "but we would like to ask you a few questions."

"Was it not an accident?" Mr. Digby asked. "Are you here in a professional capacity? Miss Hartigan did mention that you were with the police."

"I'm afraid foul play is suspected," Basil answered.

"Oh dear! Well, ask me what you must, though I don't know how I might help."

"How long have you worked for Miss Hartigan?" Basil asked.

"Since 1919."

"Did you hear anything about the German siblings Miss Hartigan and Mr. Pippins had been hiding?" Basil asked.

Mr. Digby flinched slightly. "Those were the rumours."

"What did you hear, exactly?" Basil pressed.

"Before the conflict, Mr. Schubert had been a respected solicitor, and his sister worked as his secretary. Miss Hartigan was a client. At some point, Mr. Schubert and Miss Hartigan had formed an attachment. They discreetly started spending time together because trouble had been brewing on the Continent, and certain negative sentiments towards the Germans were already beginning to stir. According to, er, some who knew her well."

Ginger raised a brow. "Mrs. Underhill?"

Mr. Digby's lips twitched, but he declined to give away his source. "Some believe Mr. Schubert had intended to propose marriage."

Oh mercy. Ginger frowned sympathetically. "Then the Aliens Restriction Act came into law."

"That's right, madam," Mr. Digby said. "All Germans had to register with the police. The men were taken, leaving their families to fend for themselves in a hostile environment. Across the country, German shops were targeted by vandals. Germanophobia spread fast and furiously." Mr. Digby shifted in his seat. "I fought in France, of course, but had to leave on several occasions, returning to England. I witnessed the hostility first hand."

"Is there anything else of note that comes to mind?" Basil asked.

The butler shook his head. "No, sir."

Rising, Basil said, "Thank you for your time, Mr. Digby."

Ginger and the butler stood as well. "It was a pleasure to meet you, Mr. Digby," Ginger said.

"Likewise, madam," Mr. Digby returned with a bow.

"What are you going to do now?" Ginger asked.

Mr. Digby's countenance dropped. "I really don't know."

Ginger mused about her mysterious cousin on their way back to the inn. Florence had been in love with Mr. Schubert, who had passed away. Perhaps that was why she never married.

21

The next morning, Basil kissed Ginger goodbye, leaving her at the inn to enjoy a bit of leisure before catching the train back to London. After speaking to everyone employed at The Willows, they had agreed there wasn't a good reason to continue lingering in Great Yarmouth, especially since the winter weather wasn't inviting. Basil thought he should take the time to call in at the police station before they left. It never hurt to hear what the local bobbies had to say.

The station was a short distance from the inn. The slushy roads, dotted with piles of snow, made it difficult for motorcars and taxicabs to navigate. Basil decided it would be easier to walk, and the hems of his trousers were damp by the time he arrived. The station's reception area was manned by a single officer, who must've drawn the short straw to be assigned duties over the Christmas period.

"Good day, Constable," he began. "I'm Chief Inspector Reed from Scotland Yard on personal business in your fine town."

"Good day to you too, sir," the officer said. "Welcome to Great Yarmouth." After a moment, he added, "Is there something specific I can help you with?"

Basil guessed the officer was in his mid-forties, certainly of age to have fought in France. "Firstly, have you heard that Miss Florence Hartigan has passed away? She was a local resident; her house is located to the south of town."

"Yes, sir. Just this morning. News moves slowly over Christmas, sir."

"Please note that my wife and I have already notified Miss Hartigan's staff."

"Yes, sir. Thank you, sir." The officer scribbled something on a pad of paper, then returned his attention to Basil. "Is there anything else, sir?"

"There is," Basil stated. "I have a question regarding the war years. You see, I'm curious, and I'm wondering if you could tell me about a particular event. Miss Hartigan, the same one who's recently passed away, and her butler were arrested for harbouring Germans in her house?"

The officer blew out a breath. "That is a curious question, indeed. I was in France at the time. Lucky to be alive, I am. But I can check the files. Do you happen to have a date in mind?"

"I believe it was over Christmas 1916," Basil said.

"Righto," the officer said. "Give me a moment."

Basil watched the back of the officer as he shuffled through the drawers of a tall filing cabinet. Finally, he turned, file in hand.

"I believe this is it," he said. With the file open, he read, "Miss Florence Hartigan and her butler, Mr. Clive Pippins, were arrested for harbouring German aliens, Tobias and Hilde Schubert."

"Does it say anything about the fate of Miss Schubert?"

The officer ran his finger down the page as he scoured for the information, turned the page, and kept reading. "The brother died in jail from complications from a head injury. The doctor's report says blood clot in the brain. The sister escaped and is presumed dead."

"Why is she presumed dead?" Basil asked.

The officer shrugged. "The notes aren't clear.

Many German women and children didn't make it during those years. Starvation. Illness. Suicide. The war managed to nearly clear Britain of all Germans, either by death or deportation. There aren't many left around here."

Basil tipped his hat. "Thank you, and Happy New Year."

"Happy New Year, sir," the man replied.

"Oh," Basil said, turning back to the officer before he stepped out of the door. "Where would someone get a hand bomb around here?"

"A hand bomb, sir?"

"Yes. If one were interested in collecting war relics, including a German hand bomb? Is there someone one would especially seek out?"

The officer gave Basil a name and address. Basil nodded, then waved down another taxicab. Checking his watch, Basil saw he had less than an hour before he needed to meet Ginger and head to the train station.

"Driver," he started, "I'm in a bit of a hurry."

"I'll do me best, sir." The driver put his weight on the accelerator, and his skills as a driver were tested as he manoeuvred over slippery sections and slower vehicles—many weren't making any progress.

The address was a nondescript brick building

with a worn sign that read "Pawn Shop". Underneath that, "War Memorabilia". Inside, a man at the counter with thinning hair and thick spectacles raised his head long enough to catch Basil's eye, nod, and then drop his gaze back to the *True Story* magazine he was reading. The shelves were filled with a mishmash of curiosities—smoking pipes and cleaners; hammers and wrenches with varying stages of rusting; pots and pans and sundry kitchen items; hats and belts, mufflers and mittens, all grey with a fine layer of dust. A glass-fronted cabinet with shelves displayed finer items like necklaces, rings, bracelets, and watches.

When Basil approached, the man put his magazine down, pushed up his spectacles, and stood. Basil took a moment to pretend interest in the baubles on offer as he scratched his neck.

"Yer lookin' for somethin' special for the missus?" The man pushed a pad of paper and a pencil across the countertop. "'Fraid I'm deaf as a post. Blasted war."

Basil picked up the pencil, speaking aloud as he wrote. "I'm looking for something rather specific. The sign in the window says you deal in war memorabilia." Basil showed the man his police identification, then continued to scribble. "Do you sell

German-made hand bombs? Have you sold one recently?"

"I only sell what folks bring my way," the man said. "Nothin' illegal, like."

"I got your name from the local police," Basil scratched quickly. "You aren't in trouble. I'm just looking for information."

"As a matter o' fact, I did sell a German 'and bomb a while back. To a strange lady. Not my business what she wanted it for, and I dinn't ask."

"What did the lady look like?" Basil asked as he scribbled.

The man wrinkled his nose. "Well, let's see. My memory's not so good as it used to be."

Basil stared back. "You're not asking for a bribe, are you?" He didn't write the question out, but the man seemed able to read his lips.

"No, sir. No, sir! I'm tellin' yer the truth." He knocked on his head. "The noggin's full of wood."

Basil wrote, "What did she look like?"

"Er, she wasn't so short or so tall. Not so old, not so young. Wore a scarf, see, so I couldn't see her hair colour. Dressed plainly, not so poor, not so rich."

Basil narrowed his eyes in frustration, then scribbled, "Was there anything about the woman that wasn't average?"

The man shrugged. "She passed me a note before I could even tell her I don't hear well, like a character in *The Great Impersonation*."

Basil was surprised that this man had read E. Phillips Oppenheim's popular spy book. One truly must not judge a book by its cover.

"Do you still have the note?" Basil asked as he wrote the question.

"I think so, yes." The man opened a drawer, dug around, and pulled out a small note.

Basil read it and frowned. The handwriting looked much like the handwriting of the riddle found in Florence Hartigan's handbag.

"Do you mind if I take this?" Basil asked. And at the man's look of disappointment, he wrote, "I'll give you a police receipt."

The man's countenance cheered as he held out a palm. "A pleasure doin' business with yer, sir."

When Basil returned to the inn, he found Ginger packed and ready to go. She pointed to her wrist-watch. "You're cutting it close."

"I held the taxicab." Basil requested help from the porter to load their luggage as he paid the final tally to the cheerful Mr. Watts.

"Sorry to see you fine folks leaving so soon," he said.

"Our business here ended sooner than we thought," Basil said. "We're eager to return to our family in London for the New Year celebrations."

"I wish you happy travels," Mr. Watts said.

The taxicab ride was a mix of hanging on for dear life through slippery and slushy road conditions as the vehicle jerked this way and that, and anxiety driven by times of idling behind horses letting their drivers know in no uncertain terms that they didn't like trotting through puddles. Basil repeatedly checked his watch, worried they'd miss the train's departure.

He needn't have worried as the weather had caused departure delays, and he and Ginger had plenty of time to board the train to Norwich and finally discuss Basil's discovery.

"A mystery woman?" Ginger said.

Basil showed her the note, adding with a bemused grin, "This cost me a sixpense."

"I see the similarities to the riddle we found in cousin Florence's handbag," Ginger said. "Who could it be?"

"What were your thoughts about the maid, Penny?" Basil asked.

"She seemed very uncomfortable with my questions," Ginger answered, "and it is rather convenient that she was in London, and at Hatchards, during the same period her mistress was there."

"London is a big city," Basil countered. "Many people have relatives living there whom they visited for Christmas."

"Could it be Mrs. Underhill?" Ginger offered. "Perhaps she disapproved, resented being pulled into the scheme, which I'm certain she must have been."

"But why now?" Basil asked. "So many years after the fact."

"Had cousin Florence given her notice?" Ginger asked. "If that came without a reference due to a falling out, it would be difficult for the cook to get another position."

"The same scenario could be true for Penny," Basil said.

"The two of them could've planned this together," Ginger offered. "Mrs. Underhill obtained the hand bomb—a German one would be rather poetic, under the circumstances—and Penny planted it in the shop."

"Penny would have had to hide from Mr. Jennings when he locked the shop up," Basil said. "She would've had all night to rig the bomb, then could've acted like an early customer in the morning.

"It's an elaborate plan," Ginger said, "but rather

ingenious. Causing their mistress's demise in another city. It really distances them from the crime."

"When I get back to the Yard, I'll arrange for a deeper look into both of those women," Basil said.

Ginger gazed out the window, the afternoon growing dark. Their image in the glass reflected them —him, handsome, wearing his trilby, with notes of grey at his temples, and her in her fur hat, her lips forming a smile of contentment.

22

The next morning, Hartigan House was abuzz with activity as Ginger oversaw preparations for the New Year's Eve party scheduled for the following night. There had been times over the previous few days that Ginger had thought she'd be forced to cancel the event due to the weather, but thankfully the snowfall had turned to rain. Lizzie and Grace were busy dusting and adding final decorations. Mrs. Beasley was cooking like a madwoman in the kitchen. And Felicia assisted as well by overseeing and directing affairs.

Ginger joined Felicia in the drawing room, pleased that everything was bright, clean, and ready for the party. The conversation quickly turned to gala attire.

"I love the gown Emma made for me," Felicia gushed.

"I can't wait to see it," Ginger replied. "She created mine for me as well."

"Such a talent," Felicia returned. "You're lucky to have her."

"I'm aware of that." Ginger exhaled dramatically. "I dread the day when she launches out on her own."

"Oh, you'll snap up another young thing who's equally talented," Felicia said, "though it's not anything you have to worry about for a while. Emma adores you."

Ambrosia's entry into the drawing room was announced by the tapping of her walking stick on the tiles. She blustered through wrinkled lips, "How are we to manage so many guests in the house without a butler?" Her bulbous eyes studied Ginger. "Have you found another man?"

Ginger bristled at replacing Pippins, her thoughts on the poor man.

"Georgia!" Ambrosia often reverted to Ginger's Christian name when upset. "I won't be ignored."

"I'm dreadfully sorry, Grandmother. My mind is in a million places at once. I've employed a temporary man to take care of butler duties." Ginger patted

Ambrosia's arm. "Don't worry. Everything will go smoothly."

Ginger started through the entrance hall just as Haley, dressed for the outdoors, descended the staircase. "No rest for the wicked," Ginger said with a smile.

"Dr. Palmer has invited me to participate in a post-mortem today. I suspect it's a heart attack, but the family wants to know for sure."

"A heart attack?" Ginger raised a brow. "Hardly a challenge for you."

Haley shrugged. "I won't say no to more experience. When a man makes room for a woman in his field, it's not something to take lightly."

Ginger wondered if Dr. Palmer's charm and boyish good looks had anything to do with Haley's enthusiasm, but she wisely kept such thoughts to herself. "I'll soon be heading to the hospital myself," she said. "I could give you a lift."

"Not necessary," Haley said quickly. "I'm in a hurry, and I've already called a taxicab."

BY THE NEXT DAY, the main roads had been cleared, and despite heavy rain—and what Londoner allowed a bit of rain to keep them from doing what they must

LEE STRAUSS

—Ginger drove her Crossley the short way across the city to St. Bartholomew's. She was pleased to find Pippins sitting up in bed, his cornflower-blue eyes watery but alert.

"Pips!"

With his one good arm, Pippins shifted into a higher sitting position. "Mrs. Reed. It's so good of you to come."

"I wanted to see you. I've been here a few times."

"The nurses have mentioned it. That's so kind of you, madam."

"I'm so thrilled to see you awake and of sound mind."

He smiled slyly. "Well, I am awake, madam."

Ginger laughed at his self-deprecating humour. She reached for his hand, then said soberly, "Have they told you about poor Miss Hartigan?"

Pippins' expression darkened. "Yes, madam. I was terribly sorry to hear about it. Have you learned what happened?"

"Mr. Reed is investigating, and I'm asking around." Ginger patted Pippins' arm. "In fact, we got back from a short trip to The Willows a couple of days ago."

"Is that so?" Pippins worked his lips. "What did you discover there?"

"Nothing conclusive, I'm afraid. We spoke to the staff: Mrs. Underhill, the maid, Penny, and Mr. Digby, the new butler."

Pippins nodded, acknowledging that he was acquainted with the names, but said nothing.

Ginger continued, "They spoke of the German siblings that you and Miss Hartigan hid in the secret room."

Pippins grunted. "That's not so secret anymore."

"Not since the police raided the house in 1916," Ginger confirmed. "I'd love to hear the story from your point of view."

Pippins rested his blue-eyed gaze on her. "Do you think it has something to do with the blast at the bookshop?"

"Quite honestly, I don't know. All I know is that you were at Hatchards that day and at that time at the behest of Miss Hartigan, weren't you?"

"Yes, madam."

"And we have reason to believe she was lured there, but we can't ascertain by whom. Perhaps there will be a clue in your recollection of events." Not to mention that his dreams, while unconscious, seemed to centre around those times.

"Very well, madam," Pippins said. He rested his head on the stack of pillows and inhaled deeply

187

before starting. "It began, as you know, when your father decided to shut up Hartigan House. I took a bedsit in London, wondering what to do with myself, scouring the newspapers for new employment. I went to a few interviews but didn't find a fit." He smiled at Ginger. "The Hartigan family was a hard act to follow. Your father had given me a healthy severance, so I wasn't in dire straits and had the luxury of taking my time. Then I received word from Mr. Hartigan that he'd like me to work for Miss Florence Hartigan, his spinster cousin. He perceived that trouble was brewing in Europe and didn't want his single female relation to face it alone."

"My father must've been aware that Miss Hartigan had staff on hand," Ginger said. "She wasn't truly alone."

"Perhaps your father wanted someone he could trust, who could report back to him." He frowned as he let out a heavy sigh. "Clearly, I failed him."

Ginger patted his hand. "Father mustn't have thought that, as he welcomed you back to Hartigan House."

"Your father was a gracious man, madam."

Ginger quite agreed and speaking of him made her heart pinch. She still missed him dearly.

"Was Miss Hartigan agreeable to the appointment?"

"I must admit that my welcome wasn't warm, but I grew on her over time."

"When she needed your help," Ginger said.

"Quite so."

"What were your impressions of the staff?" Ginger asked. More to the point, had any of them shown signs of latent violence? But Ginger was careful not to direct Pippins' response.

"They were all most certainly loyal to Miss Hartigan," Pippins said.

"At what point did Miss Hartigan bring you in on her plan to hide the German siblings?"

"When I confronted her, she immediately brought me on board to assist. Only Mrs. Underhill was aware of the subterfuge."

"She gave you no choice?" Ginger asked.

"What choice was there, madam?" Pippins said. "Once I knew, I was complicit. Besides, I could see that she was in over her head. She wasn't built to handle life's demands and hardships. I couldn't leave her on her own."

If Ginger hadn't already loved Pippins, she would have been smitten at that point. "You're a good man, Pips."

"That's kind of you to say, madam. Would you mind passing me that glass of water?"

Ginger did as requested, and after Pippins wet his lips, she waited for him to start again.

"Over time, we fell into a routine. I ordered more food than we needed, and Miss Hartigan and I ate less than our portions."

"I've learned the siblings were called Schubert. What were they like?"

"Mr. Schubert was a gentle soul and obviously taken with Miss Hartigan. There was no question the feeling was mutual. This bond drove Miss Hartigan to break the law. My impression of Miss Schubert was that she'd gone through life more intelligently than her peers but was not respected for it because of her sex. She consumed every book we could sneak up to her, devoured every newspaper. She was short-tempered and easily agitated."

"What happened to Miss Schubert?"

Pippins lifted a bony shoulder. "She escaped when Mr. Schubert didn't. Rumours travelled about at the time. Anything from being shot in the back, drowning in the sea as she tried to swim away, and finding her way back to Germany."

"You spent time in jail," Ginger stated.

"I did, madam. Please forgive me for not disclosing that fact."

"There's no need for forgiveness, Pippins. I'm so sorry you had to go through that hardship."

Pippins grew silent. "Any friend of someone with German connections was no friend of King and country. Let's say I wasn't popular amongst the other prisoners. But I was given enough food and a bed to sleep on. Many other men suffered much worse."

"How long were you detained?" Ginger asked.

Pippins inhaled. "Just over a year and a half, madam. The headlines on the day of my release were about King George announcing that the House of Saxe-Coburg-Gotha would now be called the House of Windsor."

Ginger remembered the day well. July 17, 1917. The British monarchy didn't want to be included in the anti-German sentiment of the time, especially as the King's first cousin was Kaiser Wilhelm II.

A tapping on the door stopped the conversation, and the doctor entered. "I have good news," he said. "You're free to go home, so long as you won't be alone."

Ginger cheered inwardly. "That's fantastic news! We'll be certain to take good care of him." She squeezed Pippins' hand. "You're coming home! I'll let the nurse help you dress. I have to get back, but I'll send Clement to come for you in an hour."

Shaking the doctor's hand, she said, "Such a terrific way to bring in the new year. Happy new year to you!"

When Ginger reached the main floor of the hospital, she made an impulsive detour. Instead of going out the main doors, she headed down one more flight of stairs toward the mortuary. She knocked on the door before nudging it open. "Hello?"

The cool and quiet mortuary had a tranquil effect, making one want to whisper. Haley turned to her voice with a look of surprise and smiled. "Ginger. I wondered if we'd get a visit from you after you checked in on Pippins. How is he?"

"So much better. The doctor's even letting him come home."

"That's fantastic," Haley said.

Dr. Palmer straightened, his lips pulling into a smile. "Happy news, indeed."

"I'm glad you're here, Ginger," Haley said.

"After we finished the morning post-mortem," Dr. Palmer started, "Miss Higgins suggested we have another look at the murder victim that came in from the bombing. We've discovered a bit of trace evidence that you and your husband might find helpful."

"Oh?" Ginger said, immediately intrigued. "What is it?"

"We found a few grains of sand caught in Miss Hartigan's hair," Haley said.

"I rang up the chaps at the police forensics lab," Dr. Palmer added, "and they'd also found grains of sand as they sifted through the ash and debris that was swept up at the crime scene."

"Basil mentioned sand had been observed in the shrapnel," Ginger said. "Is it from the Thames?"

"That was what we were waiting to find out," Haley said. "Sand has its own trademarks, specific to where it's found. It turns out this sand came from the east coast of England."

Ginger let out a soft whistle. "Mrs. Underhill, cousin Florence's housekeeper, mentioned seeing someone behaving suspiciously on the beach in front of the house."

"Someone storing the bomb apparatus?" Haley offered.

"But why? Unless the killer had hoped to kill cousin Florence in her home and then discovered Florence was in London."

"If the perpetrator had buried the bomb device

on the beach," Dr. Palmer started, "that could explain how sand made its way to the bookstore."

"Indeed," Ginger said. "Good work, Haley, Dr. Palmer. I'll let Basil know immediately."

Ginger paused at the door before leaving and turned to face the pathologist. "I'm not sure Miss Higgins has thought to mention it, but we're hosting a New Year's Eve party tonight. Will you come?"

A look was shared between Haley and Dr. Palmer that Ginger didn't dare try to interpret. After a beat, Dr. Palmer said, "It would be my pleasure, Mrs. Reed. Thank you."

*a*s the weather moved from snow to rain, the danger of flooding became the next nemesis of London citizens. However, days of being cooped up due to snow had made the guests on Ginger's list daring, choosing to brave the wet consequences to attend her party and bring in 1928 with good cheer.

Ginger couldn't have been more delighted with the turnout. Her family members were counted— Basil, Ambrosia, Felicia, and Haley, who looked delightfully feminine in the Jean Patou frock Ginger had insisted she borrow. The dinner gown was made of thin velour, and the saffron-yellow colour accentuated Haley's glossy dark hair, pinned up into a faux bob with jewelled hairpins. The gown's neckline draped in folds over her bosom, and a prominent matching bow sat centre-front, low on the hips. Fashions had changed in recent years, narrowing the bodice to be slightly more form-fitting with shorter hemlines that landed just below the knees.

Charles had yet to join them. Felicia, sipped her sidecar, which hadn't mellowed the tension she carried in her unsmiling face, though she remained lovely to look upon, dressed exquisitely in a pale pink gown that hung from her pale shoulders by thin straps and dripped over her feminine physique like a waterfall,

Ginger spotted her staff from Feathers & Flair mingling about the drawing room, dressed in the latest fashions found in her shop. Emma and Dorothy arrived together, Millie came with Constable Braxton, and Madame Roux had her unofficial beau, Inspector Sanders, on her arm. Ginger smiled at the unlikely couple and wondered if wedding bells would ever ring for them. Members of the Metropolitan Police—colleagues and friends of Basil—were in the midst, along with socialites Ginger rarely encountered apart from at parties such as this one. Only Magna Jones had declined her invitation. Ginger wasn't too surprised. Her raven-haired assistant at Lady Gold Investigations was eccentric at best and preferred her own company to crowds.

Ginger ensured that the drink flowed freely, and soon none of the upper-class guests with a tendency towards snobbery cared that people like Reverend Oliver and Matilda Hill were part of their company. An equal number of handsome suits and cocktail dresses balanced out the black coat-tails and gorgeous gowns. Ginger had chosen something that could be considered either a gown or a cocktail dress, a shimmery midnight-blue number embroidered with sparkly sequins, designed by Madeleine Vionnet. The sleeveless creation had a neckline that turned into a choker around the neck, exposing Ginger's upper and mid-back. A sheer blue band like a small shawl was wrapped around her hips, with the ends folded and hanging. The hemline hung in waves and when she glided across the floor, Ginger felt as if she were walking along the wake of a mythical ocean. Long teardrop pearl-and-diamond earrings were snapped onto her earlobes and playfully swung as she swayed to the music from the live three-piece jazz band set up by the baby grand.

Ginger checked her wristwatch, a dainty piece encrusted in diamonds, then nodded at the lead band member. It was nearing ten o'clock and time for dancing.

When the band played, Ginger grabbed Basil's hand and danced. Her friendship with Basil had begun on the dance floor in a lounge on the SS *Rosa*, where they met on a journey from Boston to Liverpool. Their example encouraged others to join them on the dance floor, including, to Ginger's delight, Haley and a dapper-looking Dr. Palmer. Soon, the floor was filled with couples doing the Charleston.

Basil guided Ginger towards the wall when the music ended, and Ginger felt her husband's warm breath in her ear. "Your party seems to be a big success."

"And with Pips home and on the mend," Ginger gushed, "it couldn't be a happier way to bring in 1928."

Pippins had been set up in his bed upstairs, and the maids had been instructed to see him on a regular rotation to ensure he was cared for and comfortable during the party hours.

"Our social circle is certainly larger than I imagined, and it seems everyone came despite the weather," Basil said as he eyed the crowded room. "I don't believe I know everyone here."

Ginger scanned the area, noting that she didn't

know everyone either. "I did allow singles to bring a guest," she said. Fleetingly, she caught a familiar face coming out of the drawing room. "Wait. Was that the saleslady from Hatchards?" She lifted her chin to stare up at Basil. "What was her name again? Gibbons?"

"Miss Glenda Gibbons, as I recall." Basil's expression grew sober. "Is she here?"

"I think I saw her," Ginger said, "but it could've been a doppelgänger. One's appearance can drastically change when one gets dolled up."

Ginger's gaze landed on Felicia, who wore her wristwatch outside her long black gloves, her expression deepening with worry as she repeatedly glanced at the time. The pout on her face didn't suit the glamour of her cocktail dress.

"Poor Felicia," Ginger said. "I do hope Charles gets here before midnight. The poor duck has had such a trying year already. I can't bear to see her bring in the new one in tears. I'm going to see if I can cheer her up."

Ginger had difficulty crossing the room as her guests, on seeing her pass by, would stretch out their arms and, with drink-induced joviality, gush with praise.

"Fabulous party, darling."

Ginger smiled. "Thank you, dear."

"You look exquisite."

"As do you," Ginger returned politely. "Your gown is stunning."

"I do love what you've done with the place."

Another smile. "It was a pleasure to redecorate."

Felicia, whose smile looked forced, said, "Running the gauntlet across your own drawing room, Ginger. Well done."

"Diplomacy is a useful skill to have in one's arsenal," Ginger returned. "Now, what's with the long face?"

"I don't have a long face," Felicia protested. "I'm just waiting for Charles. What on earth is taking him so long?"

"Did he say where he was going?" Ginger asked.

"To meet with one of his blue-blooded chums from the House of Lords. Apparently, there was a matter of urgency that couldn't wait one day."

A chum or a government connection? Though Basil had shown signs of suspecting Ginger's intrigue-filled past, Felicia had, so far, remained clueless about her husband's second life.

Ginger glanced at her wristwatch, which read a few minutes past eleven. Charles was pushing it close. It wouldn't do for him to miss counting in the new year with his new wife when she was in a fragile state of mind. Thankfully, the French doors to the drawing room opened at that moment, and Charles Davenport-Witt stepped inside. The earl was unquestionably handsome in his black-tie ensemble, and Felicia's face lit up like a gas lantern when she saw him. Moving quickly to her husband's side, she said, "Oh, Charles. I thought I'd be forced to kiss one of the waiters at midnight!"

Ginger looked over her shoulder, catching Basil's eye, and he eased through the bodies, looking debonair in his black suit until he reached her. "All is well, I gather."

Charles, hearing Basil speak, ducked his chin and lowered his voice. "I've learned something that might interest you, old chap"

Ginger glanced about to ensure they wouldn't be overheard, but that would be impossible in this room. Many furtive and curious looks darted their way.

"Let's move this discussion into the sitting room," Ginger said, "where we can speak privately."

The sitting room was on the opposite side of the entranceway. As they strolled across the black-and-white tiled floor with the lights of the grand electric chandelier hanging from high above them, Ginger enjoyed the cooler air that must've come in with

Charles when he entered the front door. The man employed to serve as the butler stood to attention by the door and nodded as he watched the foursome pass by. Some party attendees had migrated to the sitting room to enjoy the warm and inviting fire that snapped and flickered in the fireplace.

"The dining room will be empty," Ginger said.

A side table in the dining room had several glass carafes filled with different shades of amber and brown liquid. Basil poured for Charles, who remained empty-handed, a drink.

"Thank you," Charles said with appreciation.

"Now, Charles," Felicia said as she and Charles claimed chairs. "You must free me from the suspense, and I do hope it's worth it. Don't disappoint us now, love."

"Well, yes," he said after a sip of his drink. "I asked my, er, friend, about the names on your list of suspects—" Seeing Felicia's questioning look, he quickly added, "There's always someone in the House of Lords who knows something about everything and everyone." A fleeting look at Ginger confirmed to her that his contacts had nothing to do with the House of Lords and everything to do with the government.

Charles continued, "I asked about the Schubert

affair after Basil had relayed what the two of you had learned on your trip to Norfolk, and I've been told that there's no confirmation of Miss Hilde Schubert's death."

Ginger stared back, eyes wide. "So, she's still alive?"

"Who's to say?" Charles said. "But there's a chance she is."

"If Miss Schubert is responsible for Miss Hartigan's death," Basil said, "who is she? Where is she?"

"That leads me to my next discovery. I let my friend in on the names you gave me, the suspect list, and I confirmed this with the electoral register— there's no one living in London by the name of Glenda Gibbons."

Ginger's mind raced as the pieces suddenly fell into place.

"Oh mercy," she said, her chest tightening with fear. "Glenda Gibbons is Miss Schubert, and she's here in this house. We have to see Pippins immediately!"

ime was a funny thing. The intoxicating elixir of youth misled one to believe that it would last forever until time worked the truth into a reluctant acceptance that one was getting old. Or, as in Pippins' case, had been old for some time. As he stared at the ceiling in his attic room, he wondered where the years had gone. And how unfair life could be, how indiscriminate it could be, that those younger than himself were taken before he was. Like Miss Florence Hartigan.

Still, as Pippins pondered life, and it seemed he had plenty of time now to do so, he couldn't say he was displeased. He'd enjoyed his years in service and prided himself on becoming the best he could be. He was fortunate to have landed employment with good people like Mr. and Mrs. George Hartigan, and the years with young Miss Ginger had been delightful. Coming full circle to serve her again, well, that was good fortune at its finest.

He admitted that the years with Miss Hartigan had been challenging, but he would do nothing differently, even if he could go back and change things. The Schubert siblings deserved their help, and Miss Hartigan deserved his loyalty. The months Pippins had spent in prison only sharpened his resolve to live life to the best of his abilities for whatever time he might have left.

Now in his seventy-fifth year, Pippins had to accept that it was time to step aside and make room for another to fill his shoes. Mrs. Reed had assured him he'd always have a place at Hartigan House, so he had no fear of being left out in the cold.

His fear lay elsewhere.

Pippins' body complained whether he lay still or moved but move he must. As he was on his back, he put weight on his right elbow, favouring his left arm, which was in a blasted cast, and grunted as he pushed to shift into a sitting position. The bed squeaked beneath him. Managing to get upright enough to adjust the pillows, Pippins was left breathing heavily with the effort, and a sheen of sweat broke out on his forehead. He reached up with his fingers and ran them over the many lines that had taken over his face.

The maids, Lizzie and Grace, took turns to check up on him, but Pippins knew the party below was keeping them busy. The sound of music playing loudly from the gramophone and the blended chatter of the guests reached him, if dimly. He regretted that he could not offer his services as he normally would have.

Pippins exhaled with frustration and a sense of defeat. All he could do was stare at the unadorned walls, the tidy desk with the chair pushed in all the way, the washstand with the ewer and basin, and a small mirror hanging on the wall above. The wardrobe had its door closed, but Pippins envisioned the small selection of black trousers, white shirts, and black jackets hanging inside and the interior drawer with six bow ties in a row.

And he waited.

He dozed off once or twice, as he was likely to do, regretting the kink in his neck each time. He was rubbing the pain at the base of his skull when she walked in without knocking.

"Hello, Pippins," she said, her dark eyes shining with mischief. "We meet again."

"I wondered how long it would be before you found me, Miss Schubert."

She strutted to the chair, pulled it out from its place at the desk, and sat with a flourish, crossing her leg wantonly, a demonstration of her power in this situation. It was easy to see how she could penetrate the party, and the poor chap taking Pippins' place at the door would know no better.

"I could've come to the hospital, I suppose, but this is much more fun. Free drinks. Handsome men. Distracted staff. You're ripe for the picking."

"And exactly what is your plan?" Pippins asked. He was hardly in a position to fight back. The best he could hope for was minimal pain. "I don't suppose you've got a revolver on you?" It could be over quickly if she proved a good shot; somehow, Pippins expected she would.

Miss Schubert removed a small revolver from her handbag and pointed it. "You disappoint me, Pippins. I was hoping for whimpering and begging for me to spare your life."

"I'm an old man, Miss Schubert. I'm not afraid to die."

"Shame." Miss Schubert tutted. "Can you not at least ask me why? And why now?"

"I can. I am curious to know the answer to both

207

those questions."

"I'm angry but also patient," Miss Schubert said. "I'm angry that my good brother died at your hands—yours and Florence Hartigan's."

"We tried to help you."

"Until you tired of us. Don't deny it. You went to town, and the police came after."

"We were on our way back to warn you, but we had a crash with the motorcar."

"Quite convenient, that."

"Where have you been all these years?"

"On the Continent. You see, though Tobias was born in England—and a lot of good that did him—I was not. Our parents immigrated to England when I was an infant. However, in their infinite wisdom, they sent me back to Germany to attend a boarding school. I was firmly against the decision at first. Why had my brother been allowed to stay in England? I knew why. He was the favoured child. Their *precious* son. They sent me away, and I hated them for it.

"I was welcomed back to the Fatherland with open arms. I decided if my family wanted me to be German, I would become the most radical German I could be.

"After the war, you could say I came back to

England to lick my wounds." She sniffed, smiling tightly. "No one likes discovering they've ended up on the losing side.

"What do I find on my return? Florence Hartigan living easy, like always. She never had a difficult day in her life. How fair was it that she had so much money whilst I had none?"

She laughed, then answered her own question. "Not fair at all. So, I wrote her a letter."

"You mean a blackmail letter," Pippins said. Miss Hartigan had let him peruse a couple.

"I suppose you could call it that," Miss Schubert said. "And it worked for a while. But then . . ."

"She stopped," Pippins supplied.

"Yes. So that answers your question on why now."

"Why kill her, though?" Pippins asked. "Certainly you won't get any more money now."

"I became bored of that game. I decided it was time to move on to the next stage." Miss Schubert steadied her gun, keeping it pointed at Pippins' chest. "Revenge."

Pippins avoided looking at the door, hoping the maids wouldn't arrive to check up on him. It was one thing for him to die, but he couldn't bear it if Lizzie or Grace got caught in the crossfire.

"Before you shoot," Pippins said, "can you tell me about the bomb at the bookshop? That seems like an elaborate scheme when you could've just gone to Great Yarmouth and shot Miss Hartigan there."

"Too easy. I wanted to make her squirm as we squirmed that day, not knowing if the end was coming or not, not knowing exactly who her enemy was. I met interesting people on the Continent, some who worked as spies." Miss Schubert bounced her leg playfully. "You'd be surprised about what you hear during intimate tête-à- têtes."

Pippins stared back with silent resignation. *Just pull the trigger and quickly leave Hartigan House*, he thought. He wanted her to leave to prevent her from inadvertently hurting anyone else.

His wish went ungranted.

"I went to The Willows—have you been back since? No? Well, it was my first time, and the memories flooded me. Made my chest tight and my stomach sick. I couldn't wait to kill Florence Hartigan and often daydreamed about how I would do it. Fortune had me walk to a pawnshop that sold war memorabilia. I had a stroke of genius. A bomb from the Great War would be so . . . fitting, no?

"Of course, I wanted to see Florence first and memorize the shock on her face when recognition hit. I wanted to tell her I planned to kill her and not to bother hiding under her bed, but when I went to the door, the maid—Penny, was it? Good Lord, she's *still* there. She told me Florence had come to London."

Pippins recalled that Penny hadn't known about the Schubert siblings and had never met them face to face.

"So . . ." Miss Schubert started again. "I buried the bomb in the sand, thinking I'd wait until Florence returned, but I just couldn't do it. Too antsy, you see. I had to dig it up and find her in London. And you, as it turns out."

She was taunting him, but Pippins stayed quiet.

"Getting a job at the bookshop during the Christmas season was easy, as they, like many shops, needed extra help during that time. Naturally, I scouted the building out first to make sure my plan could work there. Then, when it was my turn to lock up, I stayed late and planted the bomb. It was great fun."

She straightened her arm and aimed her revolver at him.

"Now," she said, "shall we get on with it?"

Finally.

25

"*I*'ll take the kitchen stairs!" Basil said.

Ginger returned, already in a run, "And I'll take the staircase!"

Basil's pulse took off before his feet, worry for the old butler engulfing him. If something terrible happened to the man, Ginger would be undone. He had to get there in time.

He pushed the door leading to the kitchen and the back stairs with such force it banged against the wall as it opened and startled the kitchen staff, who stared with round eyes and open mouths.

Mrs. Beasley, her stout body still as a statue, muttered, "Mr. Reed?"

"No time to explain." By the time the words were out of his mouth, he already had one foot on the bottom stair. The servants' staircase was narrow and dimly lit but had secure handrails that Basil used to propel himself up even faster. He heard footsteps behind him, Charles no doubt, but couldn't take the time to look over his shoulder to confirm that.

Charles did the work for him. "I'm right behind you, Reed."

The attic was spacious, with several rooms made to feel small with the sloping ceilings. Basil paused to catch his breath, but only for a second. He rarely ventured into the attic and couldn't recall which room belonged to Pippins.

"Pippins!" Basil took the chance of warning Miss Schubert of his arrival as he was certain she could hear him climb the steps and thunder down the corridor. He hoped his presence would prevent her from acting rashly, assuming he arrived in time. "Miss Schubert!"

A female head popped out of one doorway. "We're in here, Chief Inspector."

Her composure gave him pause. Either she wasn't putting Pippins in danger, or the damage had already been done. She disappeared back into the room as he arrived at the doorway. His breath caught in his throat when he saw Miss Schubert, dressed for cocktails, not a shootout, standing at the foot of the bed with a pistol pointed at Pippins' head.

Basil put his hands up, as did Charles, who stood beside him. Together they blocked the doorway. "Hold on there, Miss Schubert."

Hilde Schubert slowly pivoted to point the pistol at Basil's chest. Tears ran down her cheeks, making black mascara trails. "I won't hang."

Basil wouldn't argue that if she was responsible for Florence Hartigan's death, she would indeed hang. Such assertions could only make her more reckless in the moment.

"I know you're upset," Basil said. "We're here to help."

Miss Schubert scoffed. "Ha. I hardly think you can help me now."

"Why don't you put down the pistol, Miss Schubert, and we can discuss this calmly."

Miss Schubert turned sharply, pointing her pistol back at Pippins. "Someone is going to die tonight." She waved the pistol erratically between them. "Either him or you."

"Or you."

Ginger's voice came from behind Basil. She'd replaced Charles in the doorway and had slid in beside Basil. Bracing herself in a shooter's stance, her gown just loose enough to allow for it, she held her little Remington Derringer pistol in two hands, her elbows locked.

Miss Schubert had her pistol aimed at Pippins again. She laughed. "I guess it's a matter of who has the quickest fing—"

Ginger pulled the trigger. There was a loud report, and Miss Schubert screamed and dropped the gun on the floor. Her shooting hand had blood dripping through her fingers.

She stared at Ginger with terror in her eyes. "You shot my hand!"

"You'll live," Ginger said. She grabbed the towel that lay folded on the washstand and wrapped it around Miss Schubert's hand, then led her to the chair.

Basil shook his head, amazed once again at his wife's ingenuity, her marksmanship, and her ability to remain calm under pressure. Turning to Charles, he said, "Would you mind finding Haley or Dr. Palmer, as well as Braxton, and ask them to come to the attic?" To Hilde Schubert he said, "Miss Schubert, you are under arrest for the murder of Florence Hartigan and the attempted murder of Clive Pippins."

Basil had to give Pippins credit. He remained

calm, leaning against the pillows propped along the wall. He went to the butler and shook his hand. "Well done."

"I hardly did anything, sir. Just said a prayer to ready myself to meet my maker."

Basil smiled and shared a look with Ginger. "I think you can save that prayer for another day."

a week later, Ginger sat with Basil over breakfast in the morning room, eating sausages, eggs, and toast with marmalade. Glasses were filled with water and cups with coffee. They'd entered the room as Ambrosia was leaving.

"I, for one, am happy to have all the festivities behind us," Ambrosia said as she leaned on her silver-handled walking stick. "A little peace and quiet will do us all good. I'll be in the library should you need me."

"Are you reading a good book?" Ginger asked.

Ambrosia sniffed. "Felicia bought me *The Case-Book of Sherlock Holmes* for Christmas, so I might as well read it and get it over with. She's already asking me what I think about it, as if the scribblings of others have any merit to me."

Ginger bit her lip to keep from smiling as she watched Ambrosia leave.

"She's going to live forever," Basil quipped when the matriarch had gone, "isn't she?"

Ginger laughed. "I do hope so." She felt like reaching across the corner of the table and kissing him, the memory of their New Year's Eve kiss as they counted down to 1928 still warming her chest.

Boss, on his haunches by her feet, looked up with hopeful brown eyes, diverting Ginger's attention. She broke off a piece of bacon. "Here you go, Bossy." Boss lapped it up in record time and stared again with his doleful eyes, letting out a small whimper as he begged for more.

"Scout has spoiled you!" Ginger said with mock chastisement. "Poor thing, you're going to miss our lad when he returns to school tomorrow, that's for sure."

Basil glanced to the door of the morning room. "Where is Scout, anyway?"

"Still in bed, I suspect," Ginger said. "He's at that age where he wants to stay up all night and sleep all day."

The entrance of the butler followed a soft knock on the door.

"Yes, Digby?" Ginger asked.

Digby had been the first to come to mind when she and Basil discussed employing another butler for the house. Pippins had reluctantly agreed to retire from his duties with a generous annuity, and Ginger reassured him he would always be welcome to live at Hartigan House as he was considered family. Digby had been happy to take on the new position, and Pippins warmed up to the idea a few minutes after it had been posed. "Digby is a good man," Pippins had said. "He was faithful to Miss Hartigan."

Digby answered, "Lady Davenport-Witt rang with a message for you, madam. She regrets that she can't come for tea this afternoon. She says she's up against a deadline with her new book."

"Thank you, Digby," Ginger said. She'd miss spending time with Felicia, but she had plenty to keep her busy with managing orders for Feathers & Flair, and she'd promised Magna Jones she'd join her in the office soon. According to Magna, there'd been a lot of enquiries once the flooding from the Thames had receded.

The butler bowed, then backed out of the room.

Hilde Schubert's arrest had made headlines in

the national papers for days, only disappearing from above the fold to be replaced with stories of how the Thames had burst its banks.

Basil shook out the sporting section. "The Olympics are on next month."

Ginger was aware of the winter games planned to take place in Switzerland. "After the snowfall we've just had, I think I've had enough winter for a while."

"I quite agree," Basil said. "I say we wait for the summer games this time around."

"Jolly good," Ginger said. "Oh look." She pointed to a news article in the cultural section. "Madame Tussauds is reopening soon. The fire in twenty-five nearly destroyed it all."

Basil grunted. "I hardly see the appeal of wax figures."

"They're appealing to the imagination." Ginger laughed. "It's a way for people to meet those who, in actuality, are out of reach."

The door opened, and Haley stepped inside. "Good morning."

"Good morning," Ginger returned. "I thought you were out?"

"Been and back," Haley said as she poured

herself a cup of coffee. "Dr. Palmer kindly allowed me to assist with a post-mortem this morning."

Ginger gave Haley a steady look as her friend claimed a chair. "Dr. Palmer has been rather charitable. Will you take up his offer and stay in London?"

"I believe I will," Haley said. "I love Paris." She reached for Ginger. "But you aren't there."

"Oh, Haley!" Ginger said. "This is fantastic!" She turned to Basil. "Isn't this terrific, love?"

"It's fabulous news," Basil said.

"You'll stay with us," Ginger stated.

Haley glanced at Basil. "Is that all right with you?"

"Certainly," Basil said. "You lived here before I did. It's only fitting."

"1928 couldn't start on a better note," Ginger said. She grinned at Basil. "And now I have someone to accompany me to Madame Tussauds!"

A NOTE FROM THE AUTHOR

If you're reading this note, you are probably aware that *Murder at Yuletide* features Clive Pippins and his time working for Ginger's distant cousin, Florence Hartigan.

Eagle eye readers, or those with extremely good memories, might recall a mention of the aforementioned cousin in *Murder at Hartigan House*, only that cousin was named Enid and she was dead!

Unfortunately, I made this discovery after I had already finished Murder at Yuletide and it was way too late to do anything about it except to insert a quick, and somewhat awkward, mention of another spinster cousin who came before Florence.

The continuity between the second book and the twenty-second book (yes, there are 20 books between them!) is a tiny bit off. For that, I apologise and ask you to please turn a blind eye.

I'm also going to throw 10 Rosa Reed mysteries and 4 Higgins & Hawke mysteries into the excuse pool. That along with 20 Ginger Gold mysteries has entitled me to a small glitch in the Ginger Gold universe, that and all my grey hair.

Thanks for understanding!

Don't miss the next Ginger Gold mystery~
MURDER AT MADAME TUSSAUDS

Murder's a pain in the neck!

Madame Tussauds, London's extravagant wax museum, reopens in 1928 to much fanfare. The horrific fire of '25 which had destroyed the wax figurines of famous and sometimes infamous characters was news of the past. Ginger Reed and her good friend Haley Higgins are intrigued and eager to visit the museum which promises new and exciting exhibits. Of particular interest is the one on Bram Stoker's Dracula.

Hailed by some as effective literary horror and by others as unnecessarily frightening, the exhibition about the book attracts all kinds. Haley Higgins, with her forensics knowledge is the first to notice that something is amiss, and that the beautiful figurine with two bloody holes in her neck isn't made of wax at all, but is indeed made of flesh and bone!

When a series of women are found dead in the streets of London in a similarly eerie fashion, it's up to Scotland Yard, with Chief Inspector Basil Reed at the helm, to solve the case. Can Ginger and Haley work behind the scenes to bring this repeat killer to a stop, before one of them become the next victim with a deadly bite?

Buy on AMAZON or read Free with Kindle Unlimited!

———

LADY GOLD INVESTIGATES ~ volume 5
a Short Read cozy historical 1920s mystery collection

Lady Gold Takes The Case in this 5th volume of Ginger Gold's popular short story mystery series! Join Mrs. Ginger Reed~aka Lady Gold, as she adventures with her new employee, Magna Jones, a tough-as-nails colleague Ginger worked with during the Great War, to unravel these enigmatic mysteries.

Lady Gold Investigates Volume Five presents *The Case of the Murderous Wife*, and *The Case of the Blind Reporter*.

*This short story set jumps ahead to 1927 after book 20, *Murder at the Boxing Club*.

Buy on AMAZON or read Free with Kindle Unlimited!

ACKNOWLEDGMENTS

A special thanks to my developmental editor Angelika Offenwanger for making me aware of the extreme weather history in England during Christmas of 1927. A blizzard on Christmas day crippled London and other areas of England making travel difficult and dangerous for many days. Citizens did, indeed, use snowshoes and cross country skis to get around. Snow soon turned to heavy rain resulting in serious flooding as the Thames broke its banks.

Learning of this weather event added texture and detail to this story, making Ginger and Basil's investigation a bit trickier and more interesting.

Made in United States
North Haven, CT
01 February 2023

31972278R00139